Wings

Wings of Mercury

Ethan Nahté

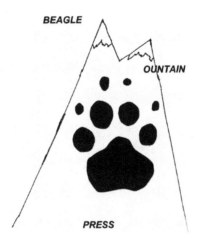

2018

Wings of Mercury

Beagle Mountain Press
P.O. Box 557
Mena, AR, 71953, USA

A division of LIVE 'N' LOUD
www.livenloud.net

Edited by Ethan Nahté
Cover Art, © 2018, Brad W. Foster
Back Cover Image, © 2018, Ethan Nahté
Layout by Ethan Nahté
Beagle Mountain Press logo by Ethan Nahté
Printed in the United States of America.

Print Edition Publication:
September 2018, Beagle Mountain Press

First Electronic Publication:
September 2018, Beagle Mountain Press

Other Books by Ethan Nahté

<u>Beagle Mountain Press</u>

Of Monsters & Madmen

The Savage Caged (Book 1: Tales of the Savage Cat)

<u>Yard Dog Press</u>

The Undead Ate My Head

DEDICATION

To my mom, who sat on the bed, playing records & showing us the LP covers while she explained to my sister and me who the bands, musicians & singers were…especially The Beatles and Elvis. Then we would watch all genres of the music-related TV shows of the '70s.

To my dad, who played music primarily from the '50s and '60s on the car radio during most of our trips and told us stories about the songs and his life. Some trips were in antique convertibles he'd occasionally enter into competitions.

To my uncle Jack, who had a very sizable record collection and introduced me to a wide variety of music that generally wasn't heard on the radio because it was either too progressive, too heavy, or considered underground music that didn't fit the norm. All hail Clyde Clifford & Beaker Street!

To all my former band members from many, many bands—thanx for the memories!

To all of the musicians & bands I have interviewed, reviewed or shot performing live over the years & to all of the great bands I never had the chance to see perform live or had the opportunity to meet.

Dick Clark—you rocked!

Music is the universal language.
It's what makes the world go around.

ZARDÜN'S HOT TOP 10

ACKNOWLEDGMENTS

My taste in music covers a wide array of genres, but without a doubt, rock 'n' roll tops the list, regardless of its numerous subgenres. Although most of the songs, bands and legendary rock icons mentioned in this story are rarely heard on the radio or any other manner of public broadcast any longer, if at all, they are the ones who helped to create and give birth to a new style of music springing up primarily from the roots of R&B, not to mention a touch of country music as well as some folk music.

As a multi-instrumentalist, a music journalist, a producer & director of both music TV programs & videos, and, simply, as a fan, music is what helps to shape my thoughts, my emotions and, to a certain degree, my actions—even if the rest of the world can't hear the tune because sometimes it's playing only in my head. I always have a song, or several songs, running through my skull regardless of what else I may be doing. Music is my constant lifeline, which gets me through both the good times and the bad times—you know I've had my share.

The universal language of music is behind the creation of *Wings of Mercury.*

I SAW HER STANDING THERE

*W*hoa, check out the pair on her," Lamtan stated quite enthusiastically with a giant smile.

He was speaking to his buddy Drap, a Pleisian, who was sitting at the controls of an older model Tresak 10. Drap's short-distance cruiser was no longer bright white. It had a dull green tint that matched the color of Tük Tôrp's soil. Grime streaked the sides and the top shell, stained before he bought it used from an older guy who lived outside of town near what was known as The Heaps.

Drap Vurnorj cleaned the cruiser and took care of it, or her to Drap's mind. He got her back in shape as best he could, but there was only so much he could do for such an older model when there was no salvage yard with a similar model for half a planet away.

Drap was attempting to catch his breath after being surprised when two of Lamtan's purple arms smacked him in the stomach to get his attention. The V'Rakkan was checking out the attractive spacehop bringing them their order.

Drap found himself staring at the beautiful female. She appeared to be an exotic mixed breed, her short fur a swirl of luminescent gold and an exquisite variety of blues. The sleek fur peeked out from beneath a tight halter-top and a pair of short shorts the hue of a red star with the hover-in's logo "Bok's" emblazoned across her two left breasts. She had a celestial body and was probably five inches taller than Drap—who was a bit small for his age. He figured she was probably two or three years older than he was, but it was difficult to say since he wasn't positive of her race. Neither boy nor the majority of any customer or co-worker had seen anything like her—rare if not wholly unique.

The *pair* Lamtan referred to were her unusual antennae. Instead of the common antennae that rose straight up or extended outwards in a 110° line and were constantly feeling about to sense their surroundings, the spacehop's antennae intricately curled and looped. Several small decorative pieces of reflective stones and metal were dangling at precise intervals from end to end.

Drap was still staring, his mouth wide open, when the spacehop approached his cruiser's optiport. She rapped her knuckles on the clear surface. Drap came back to the real world. He was embarrassed when he realized she was waiting to place the food tray on the lip of the optiport and collect her payment. He pushed the port's control switch and it opened, letting in the fumes of other shuttles and cruisers within the recirculating air from the eatery's enclosed dome.

"Oh, uh, sorry about that, miss."

She stared down at him as she chomped on her gum, attempting to see his face through the wild mop of thick, black hair. She bent over and placed the tray on the optiport, giving Drap a better view of her name badge. It read SYLENSHIA

"That'll be 18.26 credits."

"What?" Drap asked. He realized he was staring and guiltily shifted his eyes away from the badge.

"18.26 credits. You know, compensation?"

Drap was embarrassed once again. He handed Sylenshia a chip card. She swung a curvaceous hip outwards and pressed the card against a reader on her belt to accept the payment. She handed the card back to Drap.

"So, are you always vermilion? I thought Pleisians were typically an aqua hue?"

Drap was lost in the way her mouth moved as if she was blowing him a multitude of kisses.

"He's only red when he's lost in space and thinks he's in love," Lamtan said, craning his neck so he could look out the port and get a better view of Sylenshia. "I'm Lamtan, by the way."

She paused chewing her gum to raise her upper lip in a small snarl. She turned without responding and left. The two teenagers barely heard her say, "Thank you for eating at Bok's. Enjoy your meal, boys," as she sashayed back to the kitchen.

Lamtan popped his friend in the gut once again. "Snap out of it, Space Ace."

Drap glared at Lamtan. "You know I can't stand that nickname."

"Then quit acting the part," Lamtan said gleefully. "Granted, she surely is one blazing hot supernova, but you aren't even in the same galaxy as her. You only wish you could be a speck of dust on her asteroid," he said snidely.

Drap handed Lamtan his food, then grabbed his own meal from the tray. He stared at the door that Sylenshia had disappeared through. Part of his wish came true as she returned, exiting the swinging door and still sashaying. The second part of his wish was a bit disheartening as she walked to the other side of Bok's instead of coming back over his way. He'd hoped maybe she forgot to bring something they ordered or discovered she had made a mistake. He doubted if a beauty like her made mistakes. She looked like a perfectionist.

"Drap? Hey, snap out of it."

"Do you think she'd go out with me if I asked her?" Drap queried, staring off to where she was hidden behind a menu board, waiting on the occupants of another shuttle. All he could actually see were her legs and the tip of an elbow.

Lamtan laughed while drinking his Cosmic Fizz. The carbonated liquid shot out his nostrils, burning all three, but Lamtan ignored the momentary pain. He was too busy trying not to spill his drink and food as he howled and carried on. Even with his optiport closed, he was loud enough to attract the stares of the shuttles on either side of Drap's beat up jalopy.

Drap didn't wait for an answer. He sneered at his laughing friend before turning to eat his meal. He stared sullenly at the control monitors, not even tasting his arok burger.

BAD, BAD LEROY BROWN

The next day, as soon as Drap pulled up at school, Lamtan walked over to his cruiser with M'Kal, Fyr and Strahntoe, part of the group that Drap sometimes liked to hang with, although he preferred to be alone most of the time. He took a deep breath then opened the hatch. He wasn't even out of the shuttle when the teasing and ribbing began.

"Look, it's loverboy," Lamtan said. He got a hearty laugh from the trio following him. With his hands clasped tightly and held up to his cheek, he batted his eyelids. With a mocking voice, he cried out, "Oh, Sylenshia. Sylenshia. Would you pretty please go out with me?"

Lamtan had been Drap's friend ever since their first year of school, but sometimes he got sick of Lamtan. He stepped forward and shoved Lamtan back into the other guys, who caught him and kept him from going down on the green soil. They all laughed, Lamtan being the loudest and most annoying as he pointed to Drap.

Fyr spoke up, "So, I heard she had a really nice pair."

Drap was beginning to turn red once again, but this time a darker shade revealing his anger. That was the biggest inconvenience of being Pleisian, he literally wore his emotions on his skin and there wasn't damn thing one he could do about it. It made him too easy to read, regardless of the situation, either

5

good or bad.

Drap was about to tell Fyr, Lamtan and the others where they could stick it. From behind him, he heard several heavy footsteps and a voice he dreaded.

"So what's happening, Please-Me-In? Your little girlfriends here giving you a difficult timey-wimey?" Klarg laughed, his deep, grating voice overpowering Lamtan's and the others. Drap turned and saw Klarg followed by his gang of bullies.

"Go hop a comet," Drap said.

He figured he could take Klarg Dyklor in a fair fight, despite the Ynglasqlan having six long tentacles, each as big around as one of Drap's legs. The problem was, he doubted if Klarg would fight fair.

"Whoooo," Klarg laughed, turning to his pals and urging them to join in on the taunting. They did because they wanted to please their leader and this was their favorite pastime besides skipping class to go drink and party at Moondrop Falls.

Lamtan and the trio quit laughing and stepped up beside Drap, clustering around him for their own show of force. It was all right for them to tease their friend, but no one else, including Klarg and his gang of vape wastes, were allowed to do so.

"Well, looky, looky," Klarg said, trembling and shaking, playing scared. "It's the Moon Dogs straining at their leashes to get us." He burst out with another laugh, which his cronies happily added their own jeers and vocalizations.

Now a small crowd had gathered, waiting, watching, and anticipating a fight. Klarg liked the attention, reveling in an audience who would probably brag and exaggerate his exploits of cruelty and fighting skills.

Drap hated the attention. He just wanted to be left alone as he finished school this year. After that, he planned to be a hundred light years away from Zardün the rest of his life.

"Klarg, you're just a stellar-wind bubble," Lamtan piped up, his voice stressed and cracking a bit.

Klarg shot a tentacle out and grasped Lamtan about the

throat. He gripped tightly enough to make Lamtan gasp for air, but not so tight as to crush his windpipe.

"My daddy says V'Rakkans are worthless dust particles that collected in a cesspit on that smelly planet you come from and rose from the boiling pool of crap it vomited up." Klarg wasn't laughing this time as he vehemently voiced his opinion. He was serious and he was pissed.

Then he was shocked to find a very large, black hand specked with diamond dust clutching his shoulder. The hand wasn't squeezing him, which was fortunate, but it was warning enough that Klarg released his hold on Lamtan and casually drew his tentacle back. He was trying not to appear frightened in front of what seemed like the entire school now gathered around observing.

"Mr. Dyklor, follow me," said the giant who was of the Crespuculum race from the other side of the galaxy. He was also the principal, a fair and honest being who had ways of making those who broke the rules wish they had never considered mis-behaving—or at least had been smarter and not gotten caught. But that was near impossible; the Crespuculums were empaths.

The crowd parted as Klarg followed Principal Carbonado to his office. Nothing else needed to be said by the principal. They dispersed and made their way towards the school as the first bell was about to ring.

"You just wait. We'll get revenge for this," said Fl' k, Klarg's right-tentacle man. He was a worm-shaped being from Helmin-thia. He had a smart mouth and depended on Klarg to back up anything he said. During brawls the worm generally hid from the immediate danger, only popping out to blindside or trip someone before disappearing back into a dark corner or a hole.

"Revenge for what? That brute attacking Lamtan? For you coming over here and pestering us? Maybe you want revenge for being born so ugly and spineless instead of blaming your parents for procreating. You should sue them for propagating," Drap fumed, having had his fill.

Even Lamtan was taken aback by the vitriol spewing from Drap, but he liked it. Especially that last one, because the worm had no response and he wasn't about to put up his fists without Klarg around. Sure, the fight would've been an even five-on-five, but Klarg's boys didn't like even odds. They took turns spitting and pointing as they backed away with their empty threats.

Once they were well out of sight, Drap's buddies clapped him on the back and gave him light punches to the arm.

M'Kal was right up in Drap's face, "The peaceful Pleisian lets loose. Wow, what got into you?" The others agreed and congratulated Drap even more.

Shrugging his shoulders and starting to turn a light vermilion, Drap answered, "I dunno. I'm just tired of them opening their black holes and picking on everybody."

"Well, you sure did let that pathetic worm have it," Lamtan said with joy.

"They'll tell Klarg," Drap replied. "They'll be back."

"Unless they try something after school, it won't be for a while," Strahntoe said. "I bet ol' Hard Carb gives that jerk detention for a month or more."

That made most of them shiver. Detention at Tük Tôrp High consisted of a student floating in an isolated, clear cube tethered by a gravitational beam to the transfer point atop the school. Meals were delivered there and the lone seat at a desk alternated as a toilet with the detainee's waste floating off as a frozen byproduct the moment it hit the exit chute. The only company was a holo-monitor a student could activate if he or she had a question about an assignment or in case of emergency. Otherwise, the view was nothing but stars, moons such as Jen-Dale, and the planet O' Tulp. The nearest cube for another detainee would be a minimum of a mile away. That's where a student would be stuck for the entire school day, reporting straight to the principal's office the moment they got on campus without stopping to talk with others. Getting caught communicating with anyone on the way to his office would add a day for each infraction.

8

And a month on Zardün lasted forty or forty-one days, depending on the month. No one wanted to add a day to his or her detention.

As they each made their way to their classes, the teens discussed various rumors of horrible things such as the isolation cubes being smashed by asteroids, getting a pinhole and the vacuum sucking students flat or grabbed by the force of a black hole.

Out of their quintet, only Lamtan had ever been in detention. It occurred a couple of years prior. He received two months for setting off an Ortund's Quasar, a very mini version of the real thing. He had placed it in a toilet. When it activated, it sucked the entire bathroom into oblivion.

No one was hurt, but the damage was both extensive and expensive. Lamtan's father owned a construction company and the school took him up on his offer to rebuild the restroom at no charge to the school. Lamtan, on the other hand, was still working it off, every weekend and holidays with his dad's company, even when the rest of the crew was off work. Lamtan would sometimes be on-site pushing a broom and picking up garbage all on his lonesome. He was almost finished with his punishment, but he still had a couple of months to go. He never did anything bad again, at least not in school.

Finally, Lamtan and Drap were the only two left of the five as they had passed the rooms for each boy's first class and dispersed. They got to Mr. Smark's classroom, Beginning Trigonometry, a class that Lamtan was repeating because he failed it the previous year.

"Try not to daydream and drool over that spacehop in class. Word will get around and I won't be able to show my face since everyone knows you hang with me."

Drap laughed, "Yeah, right, hang with you. You have such a magnetic personality you make two negative poles."

"You bet," Lamtan said, laughing as he walked through the door to his class. He paused for a moment and turned, "Hey, that means I repel, right? And not in a good way."

Lamtan's words were too late. Drap had disappeared from the hallway, already entering his own classroom.

"That mz'bah. He burned me and didn't even let on he got me."

He had to give a quiet nod to Drap for how slickly he had been ridiculed. Grinning to himself, he relished the idea he'd have to think up a way to return the favor. Despite the fact he always gave Drap a difficult time, he considered the Pleisian to be his best friend and would stand by his side no matter what.

ALL I HAVE TO DO IS DREAM

*D*rap sat at the back of the Ancient Civilizations of Known Worlds class. He actually enjoyed the subject, even raising his hand on a regular basis to answer questions and participate. He just didn't like the idea of sitting where other students could stare at him from behind. He wasn't sure if it was paranoia or anxiety, but either way, he knew it made him uncomfortable to be the object of attention.

His teacher, Mrs. Glabnechuk, was what he would consider elderly for her race. She was a V'Rakkan and, although Lamtan wouldn't admit it, he was supposedly a distant relation to her. Drap figured Lamtan didn't want to own up to it for fear of being harassed if anyone knew he had a relative teaching where he attended school. Drap liked her. She was well traveled and very knowledgeable about other countries, worlds and galaxies.

Drap's own love of the subject stemmed from his parents. His father was an interstellar archaeologist, going on missions that sometimes lasted a couple of years before he would get a three-month break. Then he would return to a site when necessary.

That was all thanks to warp drive and wormholes. Otherwise, Drap doubted he would've ever known his father if he had been relegated to traveling the old-fashioned way in a deep-sleep chamber as ships use to travel for light years to reach their destinations.

His mother worked as a linguist. She was proficient of more than just living languages within their own galaxy. She was a specialist in comprehending and translating dead and ancient languages from around the solar system and employed as an interpreter for the Royal Prime Council. She translated documents and conversations when necessary. Most inhabitants spoke Universal, the common language spoken as a way to communicate effectively within the galaxy, but occasionally an alien would be encountered who knew only his or her own native language and some official would call Drap's mother in to assist. Drap didn't make it common knowledge, but amongst his friends of various races, he would occasionally speak with them in their native language, primarily to stay in practice. He fluently spoke and read nine languages besides his own, including V'Rakkan, and he could get by in another four languages.

Ancient Civilizations was his best class. Drap loved learning about someplace he had never heard of before. Mrs. Glabnechuk had promised them today's lesson would be about a dead planet called Earth for them to study in a solar system that most students weren't familiar with.

Drap had heard his father mentioning the system and planet years ago when Drap was very young. His father was currently home on a break and Drap could've asked him about it before class, but he liked to first hear what the teacher taught them and be surprised. Then he would go home and tell his dad about the things that excited him the most and let his dad expound upon those points. It was about all they had in common to speak about during the rare occasions he was home. Sometimes his father would even have items in his personal collection from whatever planet or region being discussed. He'd show Drap all he asked to learn. Sometimes his parents would accompany him to the museum and visit the gallery that focused on the relative subject.

If his father was on-site across the galaxy and his mother was busy, Drap would go to the museum on his own. He didn't invite his buddies because they weren't into hanging at a place for learning. It was too much like school for them. They truly had no idea what they were missing out on, so Drap thought.

He considered enjoying the exhibits in the company of a girl, like a date, but he was too shy to ask any female he found attractive. He treated the girls that came around their small group and hung out with them more as friends. Drap couldn't imagine any of those particular females being excited about going any place with him, especially to a museum. The girls that hung with his friends were more into pop culture and not ancient culture. Drap considered himself an oddball even within a group of oddballs.

The second bell rang and Mrs. Glabnechuk started right in with her discussion of Earth. For the next few weeks, Drap would find himself enthralled with the lessons on the creation of the planet, the rise and fall of ancient beasts, the evolution of the species known as man, Earth's various epochs all the way through the nuclear and space ages. He wasn't surprised about mankind's demise, burning up the resources of their once-beautiful planet if the holo-images shown in class were accurate. With their resources depleted, pollution choking their world and what was called a greenhouse effect giving rise to oceans, increased numbers of insects, more disease, and the extinction of several species of flora and fauna, man evacuated their own planet, only to repeat many of the same mistakes on other celestial bodies they terraformed or attempted to take over. Humans finally extinguished their own flame. Drap decided it was probably for the best. For being Earth's most intelligent species, humans seemed pretty ignorant and very self-destructive.

Humans did create some interesting machines, even if many of their creations ruined the environment and the planet's resources. What caught Drap's attention more than anything was the automobiles. The early machines were of interest, but his curiosity really ignited beginning with the designs from the 1930s and '40s models, vehicles with bountiful curves. Then the curves on front and top transformed by combining with the fins on the back of the 'mid-to-late '50s models, really piquing his interest. He also enjoyed the muscle cars of the '60s, something with the sharper angles and lines still blending with the curves really sparked something deep within. After that, with the exception of a couple of rare cars here or there and the high-end sports cars, most of the models from the 1970's forward were either clunky or started becoming, dull, squarish boxes on wheels.

Drap not only loved the cars, but the culture that was borne by the mechanical beasts as young humans known as teenagers created an entire lifestyle of music, clothing, and eateries based around the car. He found books on language and phonetics in his mother's collection. He studied them nonstop, comparing and absorbing the terminology and slang of the '50s and '60s eras, translating, with much difficulty, some of the lingo into Universal. Some words and phrases were more difficult than others in finding a Universal equivalent, but he remained diligent, slowly but surely getting a firm grip of the ancient dialect. He created his own dictionary as he went along, which did his mother proud.

He finally understood the basis for the name of Sylenshia's position at Bok's—"spacehop" deriving from the word "carhop." That must mean others in his galaxy knew of Earth if they were familiar with the word carhop. The same could be said about the type of facility where she worked: Bok's was a hover-in, which was very similar to a drive-in as far as Drap could discern.

One day, with no warning, Drap showed up to school with his black hair slicked back into a Pompadour. His mom had helped him cut the shaggy mane he had semi-maintained all his life, transforming his look into something as close to an image of Elvis that she could manage. She liked it. Drap loved it.

He couldn't contain his enthusiasm any longer. At lunchtime, he dominated the conversation amongst his group, telling them all about the vehicles, getting them excited as well. He pulled his handheld device from his pocket and showed them holo-images of a '57 Chevy Bel Air, '63 Corvette Stingray, the '29 Rolls-Royce Phantom II, a '53 Studebaker Commander Starliner, a convertible '62 Chrysler Imperial, and the 64 1/2 Ford Mustang. They all agreed that the man-made machines were pretty interesting.

As soon as school was out for the day, he talked Lamtan into flying to Bok's with him. Not wanting to leave his cruiser at school and risk Klarg's goons vandalizing it, he followed Lamtan home and picked him up.

"Why are we really going back to Bok's? I mean, besides grabbing something to eat or drink? Are you finally getting up the nerve to ask Sylenshia out?"

"Not exactly. Although, I hope she is working so I can ask her a couple of questions about the hover-in."

Lamtan was perplexed. "Sylenshia? Why ask her anything? She's only a spacehop, not the owner."

"Well, I guess because she sort of knows who we are. It'll be easier to ask her than her boss," Drap offered.

"Or, is it just an excuse to talk to her?" Lamtan asked with a knowing smile.

"No," Drap said so quickly he felt his words might have come across very defensive, which then made him wonder if he'd blown his thin excuse for striking up a conversation with the blue and gold beauty.

Lamtan laughed but played along with his own brand of twisted humor. "All right, then you're asking her because you're scared to talk to the boss. You're afraid Brund will march out of the kitchen, throw you out of the dome and into the bleak coldness of space."

"You know, you can be a real arok butt at times."

Lamtan winked and stuck his bifurcated tongue out at his color-changing friend. Drap decided to ignore the jibes and explained to Lamtan more about the culture surrounding the drive-in as they made the short flight.

15

"The first drive-in appeared in a place called Dallas, 1921 Earth time, and had attendants known as carhops. They eventually used roller-skates, served malts, and about three decades later, a lot of the teenage males, which are humans approximately identical to our age, wore leather jackets and participated in dangerous drag races. They listened to an exciting type of music called rock 'n' roll." Drap continued on in great detail as they traveled the relatively short distance to Bok's.

Lamtan thought Drap was going to stroke out. He had never heard his friend so excited or so talkative in the twelve years they had known one another.

They arrived at the entrance to Bok's as two shuttles exited. They drifted into the pressure chamber access lift alongside four other shuttles. The chamber sealed and ascended two hundred feet, all the while adapting to the atmospheric change they would incur when the shield opened and allowed the vehicles to park and patrons to safely open their shuttles.

"Just imagine, Lamtan, while riding within the chamber, music plays and is broadcast through speakers in the shuttle. The same music is playing at the hover-in as you exit the chamber. Then you pull into a spot and Sylenshia..."

Lamtan pointed out, "Other females work here, too, ya know."

"Yeah, whatever. Listen. So they're on these roller skates delivering orders."

"Those are the strange shoes on wheels you mentioned? For what purpose?"

"Because it's different, that's why," Drap insisted. "Quit being such a *wet blanket*."

Unfamiliar with Drap's new usage of Earth jargon, Lamtan asked, "A what?"

Drap answered with a deep sigh, "Look, we're here. Try not to embarrass me or say anything stupid. Just go along with what I say and act excited."

"You want me to be excited about something I have no clue about and you don't want me to embarrass you. The first part will take some incredible acting skills, which, I might add, I can handle," Lamtan said placing a hand to his chest and rearing his head back to strike a pose. "That second won't be a problem because you'll embarrass yourself."

"Thanks for that vote of confidence."

"You're welcome, Space Ace," Lamtan quipped. Once again, he had a cocky smile stretching from one purple ear to the other.

Drap whipped around to Lamtan, his skin volcanic red and his face scrunched up, ready to burst.

The chamber shield opened and the green light lit up, signaling shuttles it was safe to exit. Drap waited for the other shuttles to go first, then coasted out to the parking lot half-dazed as he simultaneously sought a free space and tried to determine which area Sylenshia was covering this afternoon.

"By the way, there's the girl that royally melts your meteoroids," Lamtan said, still smiling. He held his hands up in the form of tiny little circles.

Drap shot Lamtan another dirty look as he pulled the Tresak into an empty spot.

Throwing his hands in the air, Lamtan said, "Fine, fine, I give up. I meant your dust particles." He couldn't help but giggle at his own joke, his foot-long purple snout bouncing uncontrollably in front of him.

Drap wanted to shove the palm of his hand straight into the end of his friend's snout and jam it into his face about ten inches just to see how funny Lamtan thought that would be when he snorted.

"You are a dust particle away from floating home, I swear on the five rings of O' Tulp."

Trying to stop laughing, a broader smile appeared across the snout. "My, my, aren't we touchy?"

"You're a Nilsqlan vorn."

Lamtan stopped smiling. "You know I don't speak Chlundorfian. And, does your momma know you use that sort of language?"

"My mom taught me that word," Drap said with finality.

He turned and ordered his and Lamtan's usual without even asking the V'Rakkan what he wanted.

"What if I was hungry for something else?" Lamtan asked after the order was placed.

"You're lucky I didn't tell them to add lorkor dung sprinkles to your meal."

Lamtan began rubbing his tummy with all four arms and licking his long snout with highly disgusting noises. He scrumptiously proclaimed, "Mmmm...mmmm...mmmm, I love lorkor dung sprinkles." He broke out laughing once more.

"Why are you such a *jerk*?"

"If I knew what a jerk was, I'd tell you," Lamtan responded with another smile. "I just like to twist your knobs and see how far I can dial you up. One of these days I'm gonna get you to go all the way to eleven."

Drap decided it was just best to ignore Lamtan for the moment. He searched for his credit chip. No sooner had he found it than he noticed Sylenshia approaching. He opened the optiport before she got to his vehicle. He drew in a deep breath and mentally prepped himself to be a *cool cat* and not such a *candy ass*.

Sylenshia was holding a tray with their food and drinks. Before she could confirm she had the right order, Drap blurted out, "Hey, baby, remember me?"

"Us. Remember us?" Lamtan added. Drap and Sylenshia were disregarding him.

"Sure do," Sylenshia answered.

Drap smiled, almost going from a *cool cat*, or so he believed, to a big *dork* in a mere fraction of a second. He caught himself and reverted back to his original smile, never losing eye contact with the beauty.

With a sneer, she said, "Only because I remember this blemished antique you fly. Last time, I accidentally rubbed against the body and it dirtied my uniform. I almost never got the stupid stain out."

Drap's smile immediately dropped along with his head, hanging in shame.

Lamtan's smile also faded. He would've normally found the comment the perfect opportunity, had he or one of their friends said that to Drap. But a beautiful girl saying it was like a rude kick to the meteoroids.

But Drap's meteoroids must've been blazing. His head shot back up and, just a few decibels short of yelling, he burst out saying, "Oh, yeah? Well, that's all about to change. I'm going to turn this *jalopy* into a *hopped up, hip ride*. And I want you to help me with changing the entire scene, starting here at Bok's."

Sylenshia stared in shock, her perfect mouth hanging wide open. She leaned down in front of Drap, who currently was almost the same shade as her ruby red lipstick. She watched his chest heave as he gasped and attempted to calm himself. She placed the food tray on his optiport.

"I didn't understand half of what you just said," Sylenshia said in a much softer voice. "And no one has ever dared to speak back to me that way."

Drap's eyes dropped. He was humiliated and ashamed. He mumbled, "Sorry."

"But, this place needs some change and you have my attention, although you may regret that. I did notice that you look different. Something with the hair, perhaps."

Drap looked back up with a sparkle in his eyes. He caught a glimmer of a smile upon the gold and blue masterpiece standing in front of him.

"That'll be 18.26 credits."

Drap handed her his card.

She took the payment and returned the card, but didn't immediately let loose of it. "Don't let it happen again."

Drap wasn't good at reading females and he wasn't sure what to do, so he simply nodded his head in agreement.

She smiled in the most sincere manner she had ever smiled at either teen. Lamtan had to catch his own breath as he beheld

19

the attractive girl's face thrust nearly halfway inside of Drap's cruiser. "I have to help close. Swing by and pick me up then."

Sylenshia gave Drap a wink. She turned and walked away, swaying her hips to and fro. Drap thought his heart would burst out of his chest and do a dance for a lightyear.

Lamtan thought something of his own would burst, but it would be much lower than his chest.

Lamtan looked behind him and took in all the junk littering the back of the cruiser. "Drap, we've gotta eat then swing by the Suck 'N' Spray Shuttle Bay to clean up this—this—jalopy? Now, I'm going to have to study Earth culture so I can figure out what in the galaxy you're talking about," he said with disgust.

Drap was grinning ear-to-ear, his color fluctuating between yellow and orange. Lamtan recognized it as Drap's 'happy glow'.

Drap robotically reached for their food and drinks, not realizing he was handing all of the contents to Lamtan.

Lamtan sighed as he handed Drap back his own portion of the order, purposely dropping the hot-wrapped sandwich into Drap's lap to snap the Pleisian out of his daze.

RUMBLE

*D*rap had arrived ten minutes before Bok's closed down the chamber, slowly cruising around the perimeter inside the hover-in. A few shuttles were still present, primarily the rides of the employees. A couple of shuttles belonged to customers who were finishing their meals, but the grill was closed. Two boys Drap recognized from school were cleaning up the litter left in the parking lot and dumping the trash. The view of the kitchen was totally obscured by the reflective silver radiation barrier protecting the enclosure. Nothing short of a star fighter's guns or a larger ship such as a destroyer could blast through the barrier. Not to mention that anyone trying to break in would have to also get past the dome enclosure, which shuddered from time to time when something large collided with it, leaving a smudge or pock mark, but the dome had yet to crack. Drap was growing impatient, drumming his fingers on the gyro control used for steering the cruiser.

"Drap, she's still here," Lamtan said reassuringly. "She said she'll be here and I'm sure they didn't let her sneak out early just to dodge you."

"I'm sure she is, too," he answered reluctantly. "Only, I've never had anyone riding along with me except you guys and my parents. Mom and dad make me nervous enough when I'm flying and they're in the shuttle."

Lamtan clapped his buddy on the shoulder. "I'm sure your parents would be amazed and proud that you cleaned the interior of your shuttle. For my sake, and Sylenshia's, too, just keep us between the asteroids and stop before you come to a black hole."

Drap laughed nervously, causing Lamtan to laugh. Then Drap came to a sudden halt.

"There she is," he said, gasping for air. He began turning a pulsating, rich blue.

Lamtan looked at his friend and rolled his eyes. He nudged Drap. "Get out and give her room to get in, dork."

Drap fumbled for the airlock and raised the hatch. The splayed toes of the larger segment of his right foot caught on the shuttle frame and Drap nearly fell flat on his face. He stumbled forward, rising up as he crashed body-to-body with Sylenshia. She caught Drap, pressing him tightly to her firm body as they did an awkward dance to keep the two of them from going down on the platform. Some girls who were just getting off from work giggled and laughed at the situation. They kept their distance while watching with interest, hoping for some juicy gossip.

Once the intertwined couple came to a stop, somehow managing to remain on their feet, Drap looked into Sylenshia's eyes, really noticing for the first time they were turquoise marbled with cerulean. They were the most amazing eyes he had ever seen.

"Are you all right?"

Drap realized she was talking to him. He nodded his head and tried not to stare so intently. "Yeah, sorry about that. My big Pleisian feet."

"Hmmmm, so I hear that big Pleisian feet mean..."

"We have great balance," Drap interrupted, his body turning brilliant red all over. "Normally, that is. Balance. I mean we—I, me, I normally have great balance. Here, get in and we'll go so I can quit talking."

Sylenshia smiled, surprising herself that she was enjoying his reaction. She knew she was beautiful and she knew men frequently stared at her. She typically ignored the gawking. She learned she could spill a drink in a guy's lap, quickly drop a napkin on the wet spot (never actually touching him) and still manage to receive a nice tip from their sticky payment despite any clumsiness she might have planned. She only pulled that on slow days when there weren't many customers and she needed credits.

She let Drap free of her embrace, making certain to let her breasts rub against him as she turned away and bent down to enter the shuttle. The front passenger seat was empty. Lamtan had moved to the back and began sitting just in time to see Drap being caught by his dream girl. He thought it was the funniest thing he'd ever seen.

Now, Lamtan couldn't help but gaze down Sylenshia's top as she entered the shuttle. She gave him a broad smile as she made her way to his former seat, turning and making sure that she came close to brushing Lamtan's snout with her shapely rear without actually making contact with him. She knew any jokes the V'Rakkan might make later on about the Pleisian's tumble would now be lost in the void because she had excited him, too, leaving Lamtan no room to talk.

Though it didn't show, Sylenshia was part Jen-Dalian, and that race had an excellent sense of smell capable of picking up on emotions, be it fear, joy, anger, lust or love. Yes, there was a distinguishable difference between lust and love, and Lamtan's was certainly lust. Drap, on the other hand, seemed to be wavering between true love and heart-stopping terror. She found it refreshing because most of her customers emitted pure lust. She didn't mind as long as they kept their appendages to themselves because it brought her great tips, outdoing the combined tips of the other spacehops for any given shift.

After the smooth, red fabric of her short-shorts tickled the very tip of Lamtan's snout, she was afraid he would need to make a pit stop to take care of any "leaks." She could hear the faintest hint of a whimper from the purple boy and figured he hoped to get his four purple hands on her four breasts, but it wasn't going to happen.

Drap was busy getting in the shuttle and had missed the play. He was just as surprised to find Sylenshia sitting beside him. He knew Lamtan hadn't gotten in the back seat to be polite. He figured his buddy had some ulterior motive and wanted to be able to gaze at Sylenshia without having to be obvious by constantly turning to speak to her. Drap was cool with it because it put her next to him, making it much easier for him to take in her beauty as they spoke.

"So, what are your names?"

Drap was the first to answer, spitting the words out so fast he had to repeat himself. The second time, Sylenshia understood him much better as he replied, "Drap Vurnorj," in a formal manner.

Lamtan leaned forward, attempting to look down her top from over her shoulder as he only provided his first name.

"So, you boys aren't out to trick me or kidnap me, are you?" she asked teasingly. She would be able to sense if they were lying or telling the truth.

"I'm just here because of some crazy idea Drap has gotten into his head."

Yes, she thought to herself, Lamtan was definitely clueless and just along for the ride with his friend.

"It's crazy cool," was Drap's response.

His face was lit up with enthusiasm and Sylenshia could see he was legit in whatever fount of information he wanted to unload on her. She didn't know what "crazy cool" meant but she realized he was bursting with excitement and wasn't just trying to trick her to go out on a date.

"Do you mind if we get out of the dome and go somewhere

else?" Drap asked.

"Not as long as you are willing to drop me off at home—at a decent hour."

Drap smiled like a giddy child getting his first space cream cone. He started up the cruiser, preparing to lift off and glide for the dome exit.

"What about your own shuttle?" Lamtan asked.

"My roommate will fly it home. He works here, too."

Sylenshia felt the shuttle's atmosphere grow dark. The mood of both boys had spiraled.

Trying not to let on that she had an idea what they were thinking, she off-handedly remarked, "It's my brother, Xorbash. There he goes now."

The teens looked where Sylenshia was pointing at the furry gold and blue walking wall of muscle that strolled out the kitchen door. He turned to throw his dirty work apron back inside and waved to whoever probably caught it.

"Catastrophic comet clusters," said Lamtan awestruck. "He could snap a shuttle in half with his bare hands."

Sylenshia laughed. She had purposely mentioned her brother, as she did with any first date. It put the fear of Mor B'og in her dates. No male wanted to feel the wrath of the almighty god father, and Xorbash looked large enough to instill that wrath and carry it out until nothing would be left except a strip of whoever attempted something he shouldn't have against his sister. She knew her brother was really a big softie, but her dates didn't know that and most of her dates never went far enough for them to get to know Xorbash and learn the truth. She was finicky and most males she found to be quite revolting.

"I fly an Evo-98 with the expanded hub."

The boys looked at her then at the sporty shuttle Xorbash was getting inside.

Drap said, "Well, that explains how he can fit without having to tear a hole in the roof. He'd have to lay down to get in my cruiser."

"Speaking of, it looks much cleaner," she said in a complimentary manner.

"It's still stained. It was that way when I bought it," Drap said, a bit ashamed, his skin tone changing once more. "My dad says it gives it some character."

Sylenshia put a hand on Drap's as it hovered over the gyro control. "Hey, I apologize for being so snotty with you about your shuttle. Practically every guy that comes through here hits on me, even the married ones who have a wife in the vehicle with them. I guess it keeps me on the defensive."

Drap gazed up into her enticing eyes. He said with all sincerity, "Because they've never laid eyes on a *doll* like you before."

Sylenshia laughed light-heartedly, enamored with Drap's candor. "You sure use some funny words, but I like it." She pinched his cheek. She thought she sensed him about to faint, so she gave it a gentle twist and let go.

Drap was incapable of saying a word or uttering a sound. He turned, preparing to lift off, keeping his eyes on where he was going. Lamtan figured he should fill the void.

"He has a class on Ancient Civilizations. They're talking about some planet in a galaxy far, far away named Earth. Evidently, he has taken to it with fervor, even doing stuff for extra credit, learning all of their language and such."

"Really?" Sylenshia asked, surprised that the nervous boy had some drive and initiative and that he wasn't some loser. She decided it made him somewhat more attractive.

"It's not for extra credit," Drap corrected. "I just dig some of the stuff about their extinct world. And, it's known as English, one of only many languages from that planet. Earth and a specific era and lifestyle are what I wanted to talk to you about. I've already told Lamtan some of it, but not everything."

"All right, I'll hear you out, but I don't know what you expect me to do," she said.

Sheepishly, and changing a mild fuchsia, Drap answered, "You work at a place similar to what Earth had during a period

26

known as the 1950's and '60s. I mean that was the heyday of what humans called drive-in restaurants. Drive-ins were the most popular at that time and an entire culture revolving around people our ages, known as teenagers, was the lifeblood of that popular culture. They also had drive-in theaters where they watched movies while sitting in automobiles, which I will describe in a moment."

Drap hit a button on his shuttle's media player. A holo-image of an Earth drive-in restaurant popped up over the dash. A series of images followed, revealing a variety of scenes similar to what Drap went on to speak about.

"The restaurants had rock music playing over a PA system."

"Rock?" she asked. "As in the substance we build with and walk on?"

"It's actually known as rock 'n' roll. It's meaning had more of a sexual connotation according to Alan Freed, a man credited with coining the term. But the music was a lot heavier and simple than the other styles of music the planet had at that time. So the word rock seems to fit. I have only heard a few songs so far, but I like what I've heard.

"They also had some really cool looking clothes and these wonderful machines they drove around in called automobiles, also called cars. At the drive-ins, teenagers, primarily, would gather, eat, hang out and listen to music and such. Females who did a job similar to yours would sometimes walk to deliver orders, but some of them had roller-skates, which are these shoes with wheels on them. They would roll to the cars with the trays of food and drinks. The servers were called carhops."

Sylenshia was caught up in Drap's excitement as he went from meek to overflowing by the time they were exiting the chamber and entering space.

"Carhops? Like spacehops?"

"Exactly!" both boys answered.

She picked up on their energy. She was never one much for school, but she found herself intrigued about this culture that seemed to coincide with what she did for a living, learning where her job title possibly originated from.

As the shuttle approached the moon, Drap explained more and more what the culture was like. Lamtan leaned between the two, sticking as close to Sylenshia as he could, taking his time as he pulled up the next set of holo-images. There were more machines, including motorcycles. The guys were decked out in leather jackets and the girls were wearing poodle skirts. Bill Haley and the Comets, Jerry Lee Lewis, Elvis, the Beatles and many other rock 'n' roll musicians and singers appeared, finally shifting from still images to a moving picture that included sound of Jerry Lee Lewis performing "Great Balls of Fire" followed by Buddy Holly's "Peggy Sue."

Sylenshia was amazed. There were even images of drive-ins with the cars all lined up and attractive females all dressed in matching uniforms, their hair done up, wearing roller-skates while balancing a full tray in one hand. Some were blowing bubbles as they posed. It appeared to be some substance that was similar to the gum Sylenshia chewed while working.

"Bok's would totally rock," she exclaimed. "Is that the correct terminology?"

Drap nodded his head. "You betcha, doll."

"It's unfortunate I can't understand the words," she added excitedly, "but it really doesn't matter. This music is so exciting."

Little Richard began wailing "Tutti Frutti" as the shuttle turned, heading down a narrow lane in the wild lands of Zardün. Sylenshia and Lamtan had both been so caught up in the holo and Drap's descriptions of what Earth was like, they hadn't realized that he had flown them to Moondrop Falls.

Lamtan leaned forward and mumbled out the side of his mouth, "Ummm, Drap, this place is for couples making out, not trios."

"Chill, Lamtan. Not everyone who comes here is on the make. I just wanted a relaxing spot to clue you two in on what I had in mind to liven things up a bit."

The view of the silvery water flowing over the lip of a cliff nearly 300 hundred feet in height, bordered by humongous boulders and old-growth trees that towered high above, was soon before them. The night sky was clear enough to see the colored rings encircling O' Tulp and the multitude of constellations beyond them. Drap found a spot away from the shuttles that appeared to be occupied by amorous couples.

"It's been quite some time since someone has brought me up here—and never as a threesome," Sylenshia said slyly.

Drap flushed vermillion again. He was glad that his cruiser's interior was relatively dark, hoping she couldn't tell how embarrassed he was as she taunted him. He didn't have a care in the cosmos what Lamtan thought at the moment.

"On Earth, they used to call places like this Lover's Point. They'd drive their cars and do—well, basically what most of the couples out here are doing right now. They'd tune a radio in to pick up the reception of the rock music being broadcast from a radio station, a place where a disc jockey, known as a DJ, would spin records. These were wax or vinyl discs of different sizes with grooves that contained the music and was brought to life through the placement of the diamond or sapphire needles of a record player played at different revolutions per minute."

"Sounds interesting, if not a bit technical" Sylenshia said. "Seeing some of these items and devices would be a big help."

"Let me see if I can…"

"Oh, nurts," Lamtan said. He pointed at a small group of silhouetted figures led by a large figure with thrashing tentacles heading their way. "Let's fly, Drap."

"No," Drap said, dropping his hand beneath his seat and grabbing a stunner just in case. He waited until Klarg and his hoodlums were a couple of shuttle lengths away then he raised the hatch and casually stepped out of his cruiser, keeping the stunner hidden behind his back.

"Look who showed up, boys. If it isn't our little Please-Me-In."

Drap didn't let the slur get to him. He kept his cool, but he was ready to butt heads. "You and your boys getting in touch with your feelings out here, or just with each other, Klarg?"

Lamtan slapped two of his hands to his forehead. "I can't believe he said that. We are so dead."

"What did you say, Drip?"

"That's Drap. The name that'll be in the annual for bringing cool to school."

Klarg turned to Fl' k, expecting him more than his other hangers-on, to know what Drap was talking about. Fl' k just shriveled up, not having shoulders to shrug.

In an attempt to keep the upper hand, Klarg responded with a typical, "Oh, yeah?"

"Righty-o, Daddy-o."

Klarg and his gang were perplexed and quickly losing patience, but they moved forward with caution. They weren't use to this version of Drap. In the past, Drap might talk back to Klarg, nervously and not with the confidence he now exuded. Definitely without the confusing phrases and words.

Drap placed his thumb on the stunner switch. His mind raced through the motions of the second or second-and-a-half it would take for the device to power on. Another second to swing his arm out from behind him and make contact for two to three seconds if he needed to drop the Ynglasqlan. Then he had to hope the others wouldn't jump him all at once. But he knew the mentality of gangs like Klarg's; bring down the leader and the lower echelon would generally talk big before scattering—every man for himself.

Klarg took a huge stride forward, his tentacles writhing and flicking about wildly.

Drap cringed at the smell of Klarg's foul breath.

Lamtan was crawling between the seats, a flare in one hand that he planned to light and shove at anyone threatening them. He shot out the hatch and took a stance right beside Drap.

Sylenshia also exited, her long, elegant form practically melting out the hatch, gaining the attention of the gang members.

She casually stepped to the other side of Drap. She had no visible weapons, but her body was tense and the look she was giving told the crew she meant business, though none of them were sure whether or not to take her seriously.

"So, Klarg, you want to *rumble*?"

"Rumble? What does that even mean, Drip?"

"You call me Drip one more time and you'll find out you vacuous wastoid."

Klarg laughed, which signaled his toughs to laugh along with him. He started to press forward once more, about to put himself toe-to-toe with Drap. He stopped short as he caught the glare of a spotlight swinging into the parking area. He recognized the outline of the approaching shuttle.

"Scatter," Klarg ordered the gang.

The police cruiser's lights lit up a large portion of the area around Drap's cruiser. The officers could see Klarg and his gang dispersing, all but one of them running off into the wooded areas. The lone dope went for his shuttle only to discover a second police cruiser gliding in on the vapor trail of the first was quickly blocking him in.

"Drop the stun gun," Sylenshia muttered in a low voice.

Drap looked at her as if she was crazy. "Do what?"

"Don't argue with me. Just drop the thing and don't look behind you afterwards."

Drap sighed in resignation and did as ordered, letting go of the weapon, awaiting the clunk of fiberglass and metal crashing against the gravel. The sound never came. He almost turned, but he caught himself obeying Sylenshia's order and held fast. He noticed that Lamtan had dropped the flare and it still lay on the ground next to his foot.

The first police cruiser had landed in front of Drap's Tresak, a bright row of blinding lights blasting them in the face. Two officers got out and approached, but all the trio could see were their overweight silhouettes, the light behind them way too intense. Drap and his friends each had a hand up to shade their eyes.

They could see one officer pull something from his utility belt and click it. The row of lights dimmed to half their brilliance. The officers were evidently confident that the three they approached were unarmed, as they had no visible weapons in hand.

The officer on the right spoke to them first. The three still had trouble making out his features as their eyes adjusted to the change in luminance.

"Name, age and address."

In turn, each of them answered the officer. The boys learned that Sylenshia lived in Mög Nstà, the next city over from Tük Tôrp. She was only a twenty-minute flight from Drap's house by shuttle. Drap had momentarily blocked out the officer and imagined he was flying over the wooded region with small tributaries feeding the massive Norganti River, which provided water for both cities, searching for Sylenshia's Evo-98.

"Hey, kid," barked the officer, snapping his fingers repeatedly in front of Drap.

Drap was practically staring straight through the porky cop. "Sorry, I missed what you said," Drap said, attempting to cover for his daydreaming. In the back of his mind, he pondered if it might be called nightdreaming when he drifted off like that after dark.

"I asked you what was going on? Did you know those guys that ran off?"

"Sure, they're the *squares* that have been *cruisin' for a bruisin'* and looking to rumble. They *beat feet* once they caught sight of you *fuzz*."

The officer scratched his head. He realized Drap wasn't going to interpret what he just said. He looked to Lamtan and then Sylenshia, who both shrugged and told the officer they had no idea what he was saying.

"Repeat that in Universal, kid."

Frustrated with everyone's inability to catch on to Earth slang, Drap slightly shook his head and sighed. He explained with some degree of exasperation, "Yes, we are acquainted with the aggressors whom, all but one, escaped your authority. They attend our school and are a gang of bullies.

"My friends and I had just flown in and were having a pleasant conversation when they approached without any provocation. They started hassling and threatening us. Klarg Dyklor, their leader, was looking to start another fight because he received detention today after attempting to start a fight in the school parking lot. Principal Carbonado at Tük Tôrp High can confirm that if you'd like to converse with him.

"I was tired of backing down from my tormentor but was attempting to have a civil conversation with Klarg to deter his violent inclination when you arrived."

Both officers were a bit flummoxed by the large and formal description that Drap had dropped on them, but they got the gist. The first officer wasn't sure he wanted to ask Drap another question, so he turned to Lamtan.

"And that flare at your feet?"

With a voice calm as can be, and without missing a beat, Lamtan answered, "I had planned on lighting it so we could see Klarg and his gang in case one of them was carrying a weapon. They weren't standing in a well-lit area, as you may have noticed when you flew up."

"Uh-huh," the officer said while nodding. He didn't quite believe it, but he couldn't imagine what else Lamtan might use the flare for, so he decided to question Sylenshia.

"Any particular reason you didn't remain in the cruiser, Miss? This could've turned into an extremely dangerous situation."

"I'll stand by my man," she said as she clutched Drap's hand within her own. Drap was so surprised, he was afraid his expression and weak knees would give them away. "Besides, my father taught me how to take care of myself," she said very matter-of-factly, the words creating an invisible force floating through the night air and seeping into the officers' minds. They had no doubt she could down any one of the assailants she wanted to without breaking so much as a nail.

"Ummm, good for your father. Thank you, ma'am."

The second officer asked, "So, Klarg Dyklor from Tük Tôrp, you say?"

All three nodded.

"We'll see what our fellow officers get out of the one perpetrator we captured and how his story matches up. Do not get in your vehicle or move from this spot. You can feel free to sit or stand. Keep your hands in full view at all times. I'll be back in a moment. There is another officer in that police cruiser keeping an eye on you. If any of you try to bolt, you will be immobilized."

"Righty-o, Daddy-o," Drap said for a second time.

The officer was wide-eyed, trying hard to comprehend the odd boy. Both officers were baffled as they walked to the second cruiser to see what information the other officers had procured from their detainee.

"What a lousy liar," Sylenshia said to no one in particular once they were out of earshot.

"Who?" Drap asked.

"The cop, that's who. There's no one else in that cruiser. He was sweating it. He made that part up to try and intimidate us."

"You're not thinking about running off are you?" Lamtan asked. He was trying to discretely locate the stunner that they never heard fall to the ground.

Sylenshia looked at the purple boy who matched the dark hue of the night. She knew what he was searching for, but said nothing regarding the weapon. She simply answered him, "No, but I didn't want the two of you to fret over being watched."

"I wasn't fretting," Lamtan said hurriedly.

Sylenshia knew. She could smell it on them both. She just raised her head a little as in saying, "Sure."

"Your man?" Drap whispered, not sure what else to say to the gorgeous gal still holding his hand. Her fur was even softer than he ever imagined.

Sylenshia smiled. "Could be, assuming you play your cards right, Mr. Cool."

"Not that I'm complaining, but we just met—sort of."

Still not wanting to reveal her talents, she simply answered, "Call it a hunch." She kissed him on the cheek, stunning him into silence. It was broken by Lamtan's gasping noise. He nearly turned his snout inside-out as he inhaled.

The officers returned a few minutes later and found the three youngsters leaning against the shuttle, talking amongst one another about some one named Papa-Oom-Mow-Mow, a subject that perplexed the officers once again and seemingly had nothing to do with the events involving Klarg's bunch of misfits.

"The kid we caught seems to have a record and is on probation. He told us what we needed to know in exchange for letting him slide—this time. For the most part, your story and his story check out. You can go...but stay out of trouble."

"Thank you very much for your assistance, officer," Sylenshia offered in a friendly tone.

The officer was used to gratitude from the beauty of any incident he investigated, but generally, said beauty did it in a sexy manner to either tease or to try and influence the police to get out of some situation. The gorgeous young lady before him had no reason to try and influence them and she wasn't trying to taunt or tease. He had to admit she was one of the most attractive and sexiest females he ever had the pleasure of questioning. She seemed sincere and just friendly enough, not imparting any sarcasm or animosity. That was different, but it sufficed and the two officers left.

"He really seemed a bit clueless," Lamtan remarked after the first police cruiser departed.

Sylenshia smiled. They watched the second cruiser leave after the owner of the shuttle they had been questioning left, ensuring he didn't stick around to cause trouble or to give any of his gang a ride if they were hiding around the outskirts of the woods. With bright lights hitting them in the eyes and the considerable distance the other shuttle had been parked, they never saw which gang member had been stopped and questioned. Lamtan and Drap knew it wouldn't take long for the news to spread and they'd hear first thing in the morning at school.

"Well, so much for a quiet night. Now, everyone is staring in our direction," Drap said with a hint of disgust. "I guess I'll take you home if you want."

"It is getting late, but you can tell me more along the way. I'm off for two days after tomorrow night. Maybe we can hang out and you can give me the lowdown."

The flight to her house took half-an-hour from Moondrop Falls, but as Sylenshia drew Drap back into describing the culture, it didn't take him long to get caught up in it again and describe the British Invasion and the Surf music that spoke just as much about cars as it did surfing. Both Lamtan and Sylenshia were amazed when he explained what surfing was and about the dangerous creatures such as sharks, jellyfish and killer whales that inhabited the same waters. Nothing that they knew of had even been imagined in their solar system. They had oceans and seas, but those were reserved for ships and, occasionally, swimming in regions where no known dangers were present. There was aquatic life, but the sentient beings that lived beneath the waters' surface controlled the predatory beasts with telepathy, relegating them to only eating other aquatic life and not Pleisians, V'Rakkans and such.

The guys also learned that Sylenshia had graduated almost two years ago. She had also spent much of her early years taking dance classes. As a matter of fact, she enjoyed going out to dance at The StarCastle Theater on the rare occasions they had a dance night. It was seldom the music most youth listened to, but she knew the dances of her parents and grandparents, so she went anyway just to get out on the dance floor of the elegant building that overlooked the Norganti on the Tük Tôrp bank. Its beautiful architecture was outlined by neon and could be seen from Mög Nstà's river drive that was dotted with restaurants and theaters.

Sylenshia gave Drap directions once they entered Mög Nstà.

She lived in a modest condo located in a nice-looking neighborhood. They recognized the sporty shuttle her brother had flown off in earlier. They saw him looking out the portal as they flew up.

"Your brother seems to keep an extremely close eye on you," Drap observed.

"You bet he does. I wasn't joking when I told that officer I could take care of myself. And whatever I can't handle, Xorbash can. That includes Crespeculums. Not that Xorbash is a bully or anything, but he won't back down from a fight—errrr, what was it you called it? A rumble?"

Drap smiled at that. She was making an effort.

Sylenshia turned to the back of the shuttle. "Nice to meet you Lamtan," she said, offering her hand and shaking one of his hands.

Taken aback, Lamtan quietly responded, "Oh, ummm...really? No one has ever said something like that to me before."

Drap and Sylenshia laughed. Lamtan relaxed and joined in on the joviality.

She leaned over and gave Drap another kiss on the cheek, one of her soft hands rubbing alongside his other cheek as she did, tickling his earlobe. She stepped out of the cruiser using the hatch on her side. Drap had felt like a dope not opening that hatch for her earlier, but he had no idea Lamtan was going to vacate the seat.

They watched her shimmy away, go through the doorway and then the porch light went off. Drap sat there for a moment, hovering above the street as Lamtan moved back up to the front.

"Wow," Lamtan exclaimed. "Some night, huh?"

"It was *fab*. What a doll."

"I'll assume that means things were great and you're in love."

"*Cloud nine*, Lammy. Cloud nine."

BE-BOP-A-LULA

*O*ver the next few weeks, Sylenshia and Drap's relationship blossomed like a supernova. He would see her on her days off and, once a week, he would swing by Bok's with Lamtan riding shotgun when she was working her shift. Occasionally, he would squeeze M'Kal, Fyr and Strahntoe in and allow them to tag along. They had heard so much about Sylenshia and figured that her description was being exaggerated ten-fold by Drap and Lamtan.

After they laid eyes on her, they all began vying for who would get her when she discovered Drap was a drip and dumped him—slang they had learned from Drap.

"Guys, guys, guys!" Drap exclaimed, trying to put an end to their ceaseless bickering and fantasies. "She's with me and, hopefully, it will stay that way. But even if it doesn't, she's too classy to pick any of you *squares*."

A volley of bad names, doubt and jeers followed. Bits of food were also tossed his way, hitting him in the back of the head. Something fried and squishy lodged in his ear.

"Hey, numbnuts, no throwing food in my ride," Lamtan yelled. They had resorted to taking his smaller shuttle while Drap's sat hidden beneath a large tarp at Fyr's house when not being worked on and modified.

Fyr's father was a mechanic and had all sorts of tools. The boys had spent their time digging through the salvage yards—not for parts made specifically for Drap's Tresak 10—but parts that had curves or fins. Drap had shown them a variety of images, infatuating them with the desire to create their own classic rides. Preferably, they sought out a matching set of parts, pulling odds and ends from appliances, other transports, bits of materials for building domiciles, whatever they could find that looked cool. They would lay out the parts in front of the shuttle and move them around like a living jigsaw puzzle, imagining what would look the coolest. When something was a definite thumbs up from the majority, they would weld or poly the pieces to the body.

Fortunately, Fyr and Strahntoe also knew engines, because the Tresak 10 wasn't meant to handle the additional weight. They enhanced the engine and boosters where they could with what they had, but it also required some ingenuity and procuring transport engine parts they could alter to fit the Tresak 10 to increase power. By the time all was said and done, the old cruiser had the thrust of anything fresh off the assembly line and maybe a bit more. The boys figured there was no shuttle that could match it and, in a short race, say a $1/4$ parsec if the shuttle had enough fuel, the revamped Tresak 10 could possibly rival some of the larger commercial and industrial ships when it came to m/s^2.

M'Kal, Lamtan and Drap did what they could, but they left the precision stuff to Strahntoe and Fyr. Strahntoe practically lived over there anyway ever since his parents had split up. Fyr's father understood, remaining silent and allowing Fyr's buddy to crash in the guest room.

Drap now had to rely on Lamtan for rides to school. Lamtan had been bumming rides off him for the better part of the past two years, so Drap figured it was about time Lamtan returned the favor.

Sylenshia would swing by and pick Drap up in her shuttle when she was free. She learned more about the '50s & '60s Earth culture, and the couple learned more about one another. They discovered they actually had a lot of the same interests. Even Drap's parents had a general acquaintance through their jobs with Sylenshia's father, who was the executive director of The Fin' Lay Museum, one of the largest museums in the galaxy. It so happened to be the museum Drap visited the most. Now, he could go with a date by his side and have someone to discuss the gallery pieces with instead of keeping it all to himself.

When her parents learned of the relationship, they organized a family dinner, much to the chagrin of Drap and Sylenshia. As their parents discussed work, ancient cultures and languages, the "kids" sat quietly, embarrassed more often than not.

Xorbash had come along as well. He spent his time kicking his sister under the table, laughing at remarks aimed at the couple and making jokes at their expense. Drap took it with a grain of comet dust, helpless in the situation. Sylenshia eyed her brother and mouthed various ~~threats~~ promises when her parents weren't watching, letting him know he would pay. He blew little kisses to her as he feigned fear, chuckling throughout his every response and her every reaction.

Something else Drap discovered one night while out parking was about his new love—his first love—and her hyper-olfactory sensibilities. Once he learned that she could sense things such as fear, greed, lies, truth, love or lust, she told him that was why she had decided to give him the time of day. It made him nervous to know she could sense his emotions and, to a degree, thoughts and intentions. But it also made him happy that he had passed a test without knowing it and he was judged honorable.

He quickly put two and two together about her talent the night of the near-brawl and the episode with the law. No wonder she had been so confident. He was still confounded by what she thought she could do if a fight had erupted. Maybe she just decided that her alluring looks or considerable height would help even the odds to Klarg and his gang of losers. Sylenshia didn't add to his wondering. She reverted back to her revealed ability.

"Don't tell anyone," she said, not quite pleading, but Drap could tell she was dead serious. He didn't question why, but she offered, "It's not like it's a big secret for my mother's kind. But most people have no idea my heritage and I like to keep it under wraps. Not because I'm embarrassed, but because it gives me an advantage in many situations. Not to mention people act uncomfortably around me when they find out."

"A buffoon like Klarg couldn't hide his emotions or fake you out, could he?"

"No," she answered, "but if he has no idea that I know what may or may not happen, I can adjust accordingly to the situation. If he finds out I can read him, he might unexpectedly twist off and I wouldn't pick up on it until a punch had been landed. Or, he could evoke a false reading while one of his idiots flanks and tries to ambush us."

"I like the idea of our little secret."

They leaned their heads against one another and enjoyed the serene beauty of Moondrop Falls. Not many shuttles were out tonight; the hotspot quieter than usual.

"I also have a surprise," he said as he reached behind her seat and brought out a bag he had brought with him.

Drap handed the package to Sylenshia. It was too dark to see what was inside it. She reached in and grabbed what felt like a pair of shoes—heavy shoes. As she withdrew the items, she realized that there was more to them than usual.

"They have wheels," she said excitedly. "Are these roller-skates?" She spun the wheels one after the other, testing them. Blue and gold lights randomly burst on and off within the near-translucent material that made up the wheels.

"You got it, baby. I peeked at your shoe size, bought a color I thought you'd like and helped Fyr mount them. I had a pair made for myself so we can learn together."

"That explains the large bandage on your elbow," she surmised with a laugh.

"Yeah, and the two bandages you can't see on each of my knees," he replied. "I'm starting to get the hang of it, but trust me when I say the smallest pebble in your path can take you down. I'm thinking pads on elbows and knees might be wise. Possibly some cushioning for the rear end."

Her eyes gleamed, reflecting the luster of the falls.

"I can't wait to try them."

ROCK 'N' ROLL IS HERE TO STAY

*T*ry them she did. Drap learned to skate, but Sylenshia learned to glide: backward, forwards, spins, jumps and even how to limbo. She was also beginning to incorporate some of the dance moves she had been watching and learning as she embraced the culture Drap had introduced her to. She was the only spacehop using roller-skates, but within two weeks, the requests for shoes on wheels, along with the sizes and colors, came pouring in from the other spacehops. Even Sylenshia's boss, who had three feet, ordered a bright pink pair with custom flames down each side, along with her initials.

Drap thought he had been ready to change some of his generation's culture. For some reason he didn't expect it to boom as quickly as it did and found himself taken aback by the overwhelming requests for the roller-skates, more images of the clothing and cars, other kids constantly asking him to learn new words and the desire for music. Brund was accepting files of music as quickly as Drap could obtain them and make duplicates for her to play at Bok's. Her business had never been hopping as much as it was now that the likes of the Everly Brothers, Fats Domino or the Ronettes were playing over the soundsystem.

The skates were a hit with the customers as well. They enjoyed watching the spacehops zipping about. Occasionally, a girl would take a fall and spill a tray of food—they were still learning, after all. It generally brought a cacophony of honking horns, shouts and rude remarks, much to the embarrassment of the spacehop. If Xorbash was working, he'd come out and help the girl up, dragging a broom and dustpan with him. His presence and a dirty glare would bring most of the insults and off-color remarks to a halt.

Soon, Fyr and Drap officially had a custom machining business, earning enough money for Drap to add to the increasing costs of modifying his cruiser. It brought attention for M'Kal, the artist of the bunch. He could do a sweet custom paint job on the skates—and his hidden work on the Tresak was much anticipated by the gang. Drap was happy to be able to pay his friends in return for their labor.

Lamtan's father, always the entrepreneur, took a chance and built an outdoor skate park, based off holo-images Drap provided for him from his father's collection. Lamtan's father also built an indoor skating rink. Both quickly became successful. Before long, Lamtan was managing the park where the skaters who liked to hotdog and take more risks would try new moves. His father hired Lamtan's aunt and uncle to run the indoor rink.

He made Drap a silent partner, thanking him for the idea and allowing the young Pleisian to enjoy some of the profits. Drap and Fyr, in turn, moved their roller-skate manufacturing to a building behind the rink while taking custom orders inside the rink. Strahntoe helped with the manufacturing and M'Kal was constantly creating custom designs for those wishing to pay extra credits.

To add to the fad, Drap supplied the soundtrack for the skating rink. Thanks to his father, who pulled every holo-image and sound file he had collected from Earth, Drap focused on the birth of rock 'n' roll all the way to the demise of The Beatles. He knew he didn't have every song of the era, but he had a selection of more than a thousand Top 40 hits, ranging from Chuck Berry to Jan & Dean, Bill Haley and the Comets to Jimi Hendrix. He enjoyed the girl bands such as The Supremes, The Crystals, and The Shangri-Las. He dug the surf sound, skiffle music, the teen heartthrobs and the battle between the American rockers and the British Invasion. There had even been a French performer known as Johnny Hallyday singing rock songs in English. Watching "Elvis the Pelvis" had been extremely exciting. Seeing the Beatles appear on the Ed Sullivan Show and listening to all the shrieking, screaming girls was totally mind-blowing.

Not only did he have the music playing at home and blasting in his shuttle when they worked on it, but his friends were also playing the tunes in their homes and personal transports. They would *jam out* as they cruised to Bok's, which was now serving a simulation of fries, hamburgers and shakes in addition to arok burgers while the music over the speaker system ran the gamut from "Across the Universe" blazing a path to "Telstar" and zipping ahead to "2,000 Light Years From Home."

In his own personal collection, Drap even expanded his tastes to the heavier music of the late '60s and throughout the '70s, cranking out songs like "Space Truckin'," "I'm in Love With My Car," and "Rocket Ride".

Once he introduced Lamtan to Hendrix and "Purple Haze," it was almost the only thing his buddy would play. Lamtan's friends liked to embarrass him at the skating rink anytime he went out on the floor, playing "The Purple People Eater" instead.

At first, the crowd didn't get it. When Drap explained the Earth words to the other kids, his purple friend was doomed to friendly taunts and teasing. It worked out for him in the long run because one girl, in particular, named Beschuu, liked to tease him about it even when the song wasn't playing. Now, the attractive *chickadee* was Lamtan's girlfriend.

45

Business was booming all over the moon, even in the surrounding towns. Sylenshia and the other spacehops were
swamped. Drap's interests had given birth to a fad that was giving the economy a dynamic boost. The skating rinks and manufacturing of the skates kept the boys so busy they hardly had
time to work on Drap's shuttle. Slowly but surely the guys had
found the right parts to form smooth curves in an elongated version that crossed a '49 Mercury Club Coupe with a '55 Mercedes-
Benz 300SL Gullwing.

It was bizarre!

It was fab!

It was the most unique vessel in the solar system!

The Mercury was from Drap's favorite Earth film of the '50s, a
cinematic masterpiece in his opinion that displayed the problems,
pain and ponderings of teens. The outcast Plato, played by Sal
Mineo, Jr.; the beautiful and popular Judy, portrayed by Natalie
Wood; and James Dean as the rebellious leather and denim-clad
new kid, Jim, in *Rebel Without a Cause* summed up a lot of teen
angst. Not that Drap had as many issues as Jim. Drap actually
got along well with his parents. But he knew kids dealing with
similar issues to the three characters on a planet long dead in a
galaxy and cosmos light years away. It just went to show that
some things are universal.

Drap loved the images and the lines of the shiny, black Mercury's bold curves with its silver trim and whitewall tires. But,
without totally redesigning the Tresak's door design or the electronics and sensors that operated the doors, he opted to create a
hybrid. That's where the gullwing came in. The sleek Mercedes
had doors that opened upwards just like his cruiser, and the style
was a sweet addition to the Mercury.

Once the parts were finally assembled and attached, and before the silver trim or faux whitewalls were added, M'Kal had
painted Drap's cruiser a glossy black. It was the only black cruiser any of them had ever seen—because in space, a black cruiser
is all but invisible to the naked eye and considered an accident

waiting to happen. The boys figured that the whitewalls and silver trim would help. Fyr's father had his doubts. He suggested adding some blue dot taillights at the very least.

Fyr's father occasionally came out to the garage with a drink in his hand just to see what the boys were up to. He was still deciding whether he liked the modified Tresak, but he did find the ingenuity and enthusiasm of his son and his friends quite reassuring. He even helped them with the Tresak's engine and boosters, admiring what Fyr and Strahntoe had done, tweaking it here and there. As he assisted in hopping up the shuttle, he took time to show the young mechanics a few tricks he had learned over the years that they didn't necessarily teach in mechanic's school. Before long, the Tresak, which Drap was now calling Judy, could blast a flame from her exhaust capable of roasting a giant flintornq whole.

Sure, Judy would consume fuel like a blazar sucking matter if Drap punched it, streaking a lengthy contrail, but she still did a pretty good job during the test flights Drap made to ensure that the additional weight and engine parts didn't throw her off-center or affect her maneuverability. Just as important, he had to make sure every piece they molded, welded and screwed onto Judy stayed put, even after a couple of test flights where he gave her full burners and shot across the night sky, leaving a trail like a comet's tail.

He allowed each of the guys and Sylenshia a turn sitting behind the controls in an area that they deemed safe with little risk of colliding with anything if Judy proved more powerful than they could handle. He offered to let Xorbash give it a shot, but his ginormous size prevented him from being able to get in without breaking something.

Even Fyr's parents took a ride, with Fyr's father firing her up and going flat out. He executed a couple of barrel rolls and a spin so tight around an abandoned tower that Judy rattled the derelict structure's windows and sent them to the green soil in a glittery shower of tiny shards. When they landed, Fyr noticed a gleam in his mother's eyes and his dad had a large smile, the adrenaline rushing through them. Fyr's father thanked Drap. Then Fyr's parents hopped in their own shuttle and left hand-in-hand without another word. Fyr claimed his mother seemed happier than he could remember in a long time for many weeks after that flight.

Drap smiled, proud of the work they had all accomplished together. Especially since the conversion was completed after the last big holiday break. He proudly flew it to school, garnering positive attention from nearly every student on campus and even from Principal Carbonado. He now assisted the others with converting their shuttles a little at a time, Fyr's being the closest to finalized.

"Judy is definitely *cherry*," Sylenshia said, once the cruiser was deemed finished and ready to jet out to the spaceways after months and months of work. She was off work that day and had met up with Drap once he got out of school.

"Let's hit the strip and show her off," Drap suggested to the group. "Sylenshia's with me for Judy's true public debut. Besides, there's no room for all of you guys."

"Hop in mine," Lamtan said. "Where are we headed?"

"Bok's, of course," Sylenshia and Drap sang in stereo.

"Shotgun," yelled Strahntoe.

The Beach Boys' "409" blasted from the speakers as the gullwings lowered into place. On the way, Lamtan and Drap would occasionally take turns showing off, pulling ahead of one another, although Lamtan knew his shuttle couldn't hold a quasar to Drap's machine. They cruised up slick and cool to the compression chamber at Bok's, each opening their optiports once they were in motion. The rhythm of Carl Perkins flowed out of Drap's shuttle to battle The Monkees blasting from Lamtan's speakers.

The customers in the shuttles on either side of them were gesturing, pointing and gawking as they laid eyes on Judy, her midnight black body reflecting with a hint of sparkles in the glossy paint job and a silver lightning bolt streaking down each side.

Once the chamber made it to the top and opened to let the gang glide to parking spaces, they all allowed Drap to slide forward first so they could watch the shuttle in motion.

Bok's multi-colored neon lights reflected off the shuttle's sexy curves. No one in O' Tulp's radius had ever seen, or possibly even dreamed of something as sleek and gorgeous as Judy. The entire drive-in came to a halt to watch her cruise around the perimeter twice before she glided into a spot next to Lamtan and the gang. He had pulled out and followed behind Drap as his escort, parking after the first parade and letting Drap and Sylenshia have the second round all on their own.

The questions came fast and furious as the other patrons, especially those who missed his school appearance that morning because they either went to different schools or had already graduated from school, surrounded them. Drap was glad that his friends had accompanied him because they took some of the pressure off, answering questions Drap didn't know the answer to, such as engine specs, or things he didn't hear being asked over all the chatter.

He had a feeling that it wouldn't be long before the business would be expanding and they were opening their own customizing shop. Drap didn't want more work, but they had been making enough credits with the roller-skating ventures that he could afford to hire employees. They were becoming quite the businessmen.

Nearly everyone had their holo-image taken next to Drap and Judy, sending them to friends back down on the moon. Most of the guys wanted Sylenshia posing in the shot with them, much to the chagrin of some of the girlfriends standing by. Sometimes the newfound fans asked all of Drap's cohorts to join in for a picture, claiming it was history in the making. Brund even set up a camera on a remote hovercam and had every customer gather for a large group photo of them looking up, surrounding Judy with the Bok's sign flashing brightly in the foreground. The hovercam image soon became a new ad for the already bustling drive-in.

The teens were all thrilled with their kilo-second of fame. Drap soon discovered that as long as he and the boys didn't take advantage of the situation or tell the other customers, Brund was giving them a discount on their orders as a show of appreciation for all the extra business the ad and his ideas had brought to the restaurant.

Slowly but surely, other modified shuttles and cruisers were whipping across the spaceways and gathering at Bok's, including Fyr's '57 midnight blue and chrome Chevy Bel Air and Lamtan's metallic green '53 Studebaker Commander Starliner. A modification shop even popped up in Tük Tôrp that sold decals and racing stripe kits, blue dots for shuttle taillights, chrome of various shapes and sizes that could be mounted, hood ornaments—the most popular being the Fireball, a flaming meteor, pockmarked with debris and a trail of flashing fire that looked sharp. The higher-end model actually expelled a small burst of flames out the backside of the glitzy ornament.

A few other stores began carrying imitation leather jackets and boots, a material replicating denim, T-shirts and poodle skirts for all manner of two-legged, three-legged; one-headed, two-headed; four-armed and six-armed inhabitants. The rebirth of Earth's '50s and '60s was a big hit, not to mention an economic landslide for those with entrepreneurial skills.

Drap and his friends finally incorporated, bringing the roller-skates plus safety equipment, the rinks and the shuttle remodeling all under one roof. They created a proposal and got the seed money to start a manufacturing plant to begin custom making the shuttle parts in addition to the assembly. Fyr's father kept his regular job but he hired a handful of qualified personnel to do mechanic work on the shuttles.

ROCK 'N' ROLL MUSIC

*S*ylenshia left Bok's on good terms. Brund wished her the best of luck with opening a dance studio along with Drap's help, renting out a large space with two classrooms and a bit of office space. She named it The Twist 'N' Shout!

She had diligently studied Drap's collected archives and familiarized herself with a variety of dance moves. The new music went over well with both the kids and the adults, so much so that she enlisted a couple of her friends who had been in the same dance classes with her. She quickly taught them the dances and steps to help instruct the ever-growing number of students, even working out alternate moves for prospective students who might have more than two feet or hands.

The Twist 'N' Shout! took off, as they had hoped. It was great to have a business of her own doing something she really enjoyed, although Drap realized that with all his success and the success of each of the related businesses, he rarely got to see his friends or girlfriend. Granted, when he did see them, it made the gathering that much more special, but he missed the constant camaraderie. He took a break now and then to visit the dance school and watch Sylenshia teach just so he could see her. If he got there around the time of the last class, she'd normally give him a private dance lesson after everyone had left. He never considered himself a dancer, but he was learning a few of the moves and wasn't stepping on her feet as often as when he first began studying.

After a couple of months of classes, allowing students to get accustomed to the music and dances, The Twist 'N' Shout! grand opening occurred. To hold the crowd she was anticipating, Sylenshia worked out a deal with The StarCastle Theater.

The groovy happening opened with "At the Hop." A massive holo-image wall featuring footage of Earth teens dancing helped inspire Zardün's inhabitants. Before long, the full house was out on the floor, doing all sorts of strange moves. Some of the public was trying to imitate the dance students or the moving images while others just moved however the mood struck them. An hour or so into the opening, Sylenshia took center stage, announcing a short recital with her students to show the public examples of the various dances. She forced Drap out onto the dance floor along with a couple dozen other couples. Soon, they were doing the mashed potato, the alligator, the twist, the bunny hop, the cool jerk and the pogo, to name a few before stopping to take a bow.

The DJ, calling himself Zune the Moon, invited the public to hit the floor once more. The participants with more than four, especially the dancers with tentacles, made the dance moves somewhat bizarre at times and extremely fantastic at others. Their actions were giving new life to entirely updated and improvised versions of Earth's classics. There were occasions where some new dancers bumped into one another or accidentally stepped on the foot of someone beside them. Most of them laughed it off, but a couple of hotheads got into it once. Xorbash quickly broke it up and tossed them both out the door.

Xorbash was in charge of security. His skills were rarely needed that evening but, on occasion, he had to tame a wild-eyed troublemaker buzzing on "cosmic" or flying on "supernova." Both were nasty and illegal substances that ate away at the brain and left its victims true space cases. At times, it made the users very erratic or extremely violent.

All-in-all, the opening was spectacular. For several weeks after, it was declared the party event of the year. The number of classes and students grew to the point that multiple schools had to be opened, one in each city across the moon to accommodate the rapidly increasing number of registrants.

One of Zardün's music broadcast stations even hired Zune the Moon to do a nightly stint, playing Earth music four hours a night. Zune Lrkma had been the class clown when Sylenshia was in school. She had taken a chance on introducing the strange little Gorchian to Earth music and invited him to come to the classes to familiarize himself with the various dances, songs and bands. He turned out to be a charismatic and natural talent, finding his true calling as a DJ.

Meanwhile, Tük Tôrp High's band instructor, Mr. Trabe-ard, requested the archive footage of performances, plus a number of songs, from Drap. The instructor worked closely with a pair of former students, Plink and Ferozz, who were extremely skilled at electronics and manufacturing. They replicated the guitars, percussion, and keyboards as best they could. Some of the instruments were very similar to O' Tulp instruments and required a little tweaking here and there to successfully adapt. The most difficult adaptations were the various sound effects possible through an amplifier: reverb, delay, chorus and such.

Mr. Trabe-ard studied the songs and created several pieces of sheet music, which he presented to Plink and Ferozz. They pulled a few of the choice students from the high school band, plus invited Mr. Trabe-ard to play the instrument subbing for a piano, and formed a rock band, which they named The Rocket 88s. The next big dance event at The StarCastle Theater only had pre-recorded music during the band's fifteen-minute breaks from their live performance. Even though they were still beginners with the new instruments, there were enough similarities to some of their native instruments that they could rock the joint. The crowd loved The Rocket 88's debut because the energy of a live performance always trumped a recording.

Drap and Sylenshia stepped outside to take a breather from the dance. Before them was a lot full of modified transports ranging from baby blue to cherry red. Some were works-in-progress while others seemed to be the final product. There were even a few black shuttles, but none like Drap's. Most of the altered shuttles parked next to one another as if to compete. It made it easy for gawkers to see the majority of them in one place. Others, who had also taken a breather from the dance, were standing around in small groups gathered here and there, looking over someone's boss ride, admiring the details.

"You've really changed this moon, Drap."

Drap turned a light shade of red and bowed his head. He knew Sylenshia was right, but he was aware he didn't do it all on his own.

"I owe a lot to my parents and Mrs. Glabnechuk for introducing me to the culture and language."

"Is that all?" she said, playfully gouging him in his ribs. "You're sure?"

He smiled as he began tickling her in return. "Sure, I'm sure. Who else could I possibly thank? Oh, my buddies, of course, who helped rebuild my shuttle."

"You better watch it, buster, or you'll be flying solo."

"Well, I guess I could thank a special girl who listened to my crazy ideas when she had no idea who I was."

"I knew you were a nerdy little guy who couldn't take his eyes off me."

"I was trying to get your attention to hurry up with my food. You were so slow."

Sylenshia huffed at him as she quickly poked his head, his chest, then his cheek as he failed to block each poke.

"Who's slow now? Huh?" Poke. "Huh?" Poke. "Huh?" Poke.

"Okay, stop. Stop," he said, finally wrapping his arms around her and embracing her so she couldn't poke him.

She playfully tried to wriggle free, but let him keep his *manly* hold. She leaned forward and kissed him. The music got louder as the door opened and a crowd of teens went back inside as the band covered The Box Tops.

"I'm proud of you, Drap. Your ideas are spreading like wildfire. Zardün's attracting visitors from neighboring moons and even the planet O' Tulp to see what all the fuss is about."

Drap turned several different shades, emoting embarrassment, pride, and love. He stroked the soft fur of her face then twirled a finger around an antenna.

"I have a couple of business meetings with some inhabitants of other moons and even O' Tulp. Investors, attorneys and city officials are requesting assistance to get a foothold on what we've accomplished since they've seen how we've boosted the economy. Of course, if they learn what we do, it'll cut into Tük Tôrp's profits and tourism."

"So don't show them everything," Sylenshia suggested.

"There's not much I've done that others can't learn on their own. So there isn't much sense in keeping some of the ideas to ourselves. I've got a meeting with an attorney tomorrow to protect the designs and trademarks on the various items we've created. Our new venture will be called Rock 'N' Moon, Inc. We plan on expanding to each and every one of the surrounding moons and planets, hiring locals from each. It might hurt the sudden tourism boom a little, but I think Tük Tôrp will still be economically better off than it was a year ago."

"I suppose so," she decided. "As for me, my school's have all the business we can handle. What do you think about building our own school instead of renting?"

He smiled, but she could tell it was half-hearted.

"What's the problem?"

"I'm getting a bit burned out, I think. I enjoy what I've learned and the results, but I'm just stretched too thin. I'm almost finished with school, so that will help. Money definitely isn't an issue between reinvesting in our various ventures and putting some aside. I just really want some more time for us."

"I'm sure with the number of instructors I have assisting at the school, I can take some time off and let them handle the majority of the classes," she said. "Someone's got to keep an eye on you to make sure your head doesn't swell too big with fame and fortune."

Drap laughed at her jest. Despite the fact he and his partners were now relatively wealthy, he continued on with school and acted pretty much the same as he always had, with the exception of having a little more confidence and a being a lot more organized. He even managed to keep up with his studies, his grades barely slipping but he was still at the top of his class. Yet, he knew he was burning his comet at both ends. If he wasn't careful, he was afraid he'd totally fizzle out.

"Me with the big head, huh? How about you? You didn't even ask for my help when you added all the extra schools or put on the dance showcases."

"Like I said the night Klarg and his jerks confronted us at Moondrop Falls, I can take care of myself."

"Where does that leave me?" he whispered in her ear as he nuzzled up close to her, his skin rubbing her soft fur.

"Watching my back," she purred.

TROUBLE

*A*s was bound to happen, jealousy set in and Drap's biggest rival was none other than Klarg and his flunkies. They each had their *souped-up* shuttles. Klarg's was painted blood red and emblazoned with a giant skull and crossbones across the top. He'd added a chrome skull with red lasers for eyes as his hood ornament. His shuttle looked very similar to a '64 Pontiac GTO with an extended set of tailfins on the back to replicate the 1960's superhero TV program known as *Batman*. Batman's monster machine had been a one-off 1955 Lincoln Futura concept car. Klarg's hybrid Goat and Futura made for one wicked ride. Drap actually liked the design but thought the Jolly Roger paint job detracted from the body.

Klarg soared his Dark Goat, as he liked to call his ride, into the parking space beside Judy at school near the end of the term. He had modified his sound system and had only to hit a button, which released a rumbling roar like the Goat's into what was known as the Super Tempest. It was the equivalent of a 389 cubic inch V8 engine that sounded nasty and mean, capable of eating anything in its path, which was exactly what Klarg was aiming to do.

"Yo, Drip!"

Drap had just exited his vehicle and closed the gullwing. His back was turned to the bully. He sighed and closed his eyes for a moment, gathering his thoughts and patience. He turned around with his head up, a friendly look upon his countenance in a wasted attempt at having a cordial encounter with Klarg.

"Hey, Klarg. Your ride is looking pretty sweet. Digging those tailfins," Drap said with sincerity. The compliment threw Klarg off his game for a moment.

"Yeah, well, I'm willing to bet that my Dark Goat can tear up your—what sissy name is it you call that heap—Doody?"

Lamtan and the others had gathered about Drap by then, a counter-offensive to Klarg's little gang of greasers all decked out in the imitation leather and denim. Klarg was wearing a biker hat like the one actor Marlon Brando wore in *The Wild Ones*. Drap had a good idea where this was headed and was refusing to bite. He knew it would only add fuel to the fire Klarg was trying to blatantly ignite.

"It's Judy, you germ. Now *cut the gas* and *beat it*. Dig?" Lamtan, on the other hand, had unwittingly taken the bait, leaving Drap no choice.

"Hey, guys, any of you have any idea what Lambkins over there is saying?"

The greasers all shook their heads, laughing and pointing at Lamtan, who was still fuming and had all four of his fists balled up, ready to give several knuckle sandwiches to all comers.

"Beat it, Lambkins, or I'll use what's left of you to wipe the bugs off my windshield," Klarg said, exiting his machine. As he stalked around the vehicle he began puffing out his chest and spreading his tentacles. He was menacing, but none of Drap's friends backed down. They had had enough of Klarg's bullying.

"Hold up, fellas," Drap said, putting a hand in the air. "Look, Klarg, I really was giving your shuttle a compliment. The Dark Goat looks pretty awesome. So why don't we just leave it at that?"

Klarg laughed. He turned to his gang with piercing eyes. They joined in on the laughter. "You wish, boy. Let's go for pinks. Then when I win your little Doody I'll put some flaming asteroids down her sides and an exploding planet across her roof."

"Not interested," Drap replied.

Klarg's dumb smile twisted to an evil grin. "And where the asteroid shoots out from will be your ass, an image of you bent over and blasting it straight at that mixed breed you're dating. Her legs will be wide open to accept your smelly ass-troid."

Drap went a murderous shade of red; so dark it almost became black at the speed of light. He launched himself at the laughing gang leader, his fist catching the Ynglasqlan square in the mouth and his other hand grasping and squeezing a tentacle. He had Klarg's own appendage wrapped around the bully's large neck. Drap was attempting to choke his enemy with the tentacle.

Lamtan went after Fl' k because he was the closest. Fyr, Strahntoe and M'Kal each picked an opponent. M'Kal, being the largest of his group, ended up battling two of Klarg's guys. Fists, tentacles and odd flippers flailed and wailed on each other for the better part of two minutes, with the greasers taking the brunt of the beating. Principal Carbonado arrived along with two other large coaches from the athletic teams.

The principal separated Klarg and Drap then quickly stepped between them. Klarg had attempted one last punch, only to injure his thick tentacle on Carbonado's rock-like abdomen.

Carbonado shouted, "Stop now or none of you will be graduating. I'll make sure you do summer school and repeat this year on top of that."

The fight came to a clumsy halt. Not one of the brawlers had come out unscathed and Fl' k was down for the count.

They each huffed and puffed, gasping for breath after the frenzied battle, uncaring what the large surrounding circle of onlookers thought of them.

"All of you, to my office now. Anyone dragging his heels or starting another argument will be expelled."

Drap looked with disdain at Klarg, but he was upset just as much with himself for letting the cretin get to him. He hated what Klarg had said about Judy, but she was a machine and Drap could handle that. On the other hand, he couldn't allow a disparaging remark slide when it came to his girl. He read Klarg's lips as the bully mouthed, "This ain't over."

"Can it, Dyklor," said the empathic principal. "This is over, now and until you graduate...*if* you graduate."

The boys all marched to the office, two of Klarg's gang dragging Fl' k with them. They all had their heads down, looking mainly at their feet instead of at the other students that lined the path. Only Drap kept his head high, refusing to give anyone the satisfaction of seeing him defeated.

Many had seen him getting the better of Klarg.

Many of them who used to ignore Drap, assuming they even knew he existed, now told tales of how they were his best buddy because he was so popular.

Many of them, especially the others who had been hounded by Klarg and his bunch over the years, clapped and cheered Drap on as he walked the line—at least until Carbonado declared "Enough!" as he led the march to the office.

The first bell rang. Once class began, teachers found it difficult to get the gossip and chatter to stop. Drap was now a hero to a majority of students in a new way. He had publicly stood up to a gang of bullies. It gave many the seed of courage to stand up for themselves should they get pinned in a similar situation. Some figured that being shown up like that in front of the school would tame the terror Klarg and his mob instilled in the other students.

Others figured that the battle had just begun.

DEAD MAN'S CURVE

*N*ot only had each of those involved in the fight received time in a detention box, the rest of the school year as a matter of fact, but after school they each had to spend an hour doing janitorial duties for the remaining days. No one was allowed to speak or work together, Hard Carb expertly spreading each guy across the vast campus as they picked up litter, removed graffiti, cleaned the lunchroom and restrooms.

They were all unhappy with the situation. Their parents were also unhappy. Many of the boys on both sides received additional punishment at home, including being banned from their transports and going to Bok's. The only time they could use their transports was to school and back, or straight to their jobs and back home, because the parents considered that a responsibility they couldn't ignore. The exception was Strahntoe and Fyr.

Strahntoe's father had moved off-moon and his mother had entered rehab, basically abandoning their son. Since he was crashing at Fyr's house, his surrogate parents imparted the same punishment on him as their own son. Fyr's mother, adding to their shame, flew them both to school.

Drap moved about like an automaton as he picked up a dirty napkin. He was trying to wrap his head around being considered CEO of Rock 'N' Moon, Inc. It had been his attorney's idea, claiming that Drap had done the majority of the work to bring the Earth phenomenon to the attention of everyone attending the meeting. The company was making money left and right, so he should be the one to head the corporation and its many branches. The other businessmen were thinking on it and were expected to have an answer in two weeks when they would meet once more.

Meanwhile, here was the potential CEO in detention and mopping a floor covered in a wide array of wadded up homework, condiment stains and grease. He caught a glimpse of Fl' k slithering by at the far end of the commissary. The little worm purposely dropped a wad of paper while shooting Drap a dirty look, but he kept on moving.

Drap wasn't certain if Fl' k was just being a square and littering to add to Drap's work or if there was something special about the paper crumpled up in a ball. He kept mopping, discretely making his way across the room, just in case the principal or a teacher was watching. He bent over and picked up the paper. He tentatively opened it.

Tonite as Zardün faces O' Tulp. V'fin Belt, the orunge ring. Chickie run four pinks. You don't show then your gonna regret it! I promis.

Drap shook his head. "Amazing that he's about to graduate. He can't even spell and his grammar is horrid."

Drap wadded the paper back up and shoved it in his pocket. He finished cleaning the commissary so he could go home and change into clothes that weren't soaked in sweat and cleaning chemicals. Then he'd swing by The Twist 'N' Shout! to pick up Sylenshia. His parents had understood the situation between Drap and Klarg. They understood he had work to do and a business to operate. To their way of thinking, if Drap was busy working, then he wouldn't be out getting into trouble.

Once at home, he took a moment and messaged his buddies to let them know the score regarding the challenge proposed in the threatening note. Fyr replied that he'd be there and would pick up any of the others who needed a lift. They all agreed to go. They knew if they got caught by their folks that their punishment would be increased, but they felt they owed allegiance and support to their buddy.

Drap made it to the dance hall. After the last of her students left, he explained the situation to Sylenshia.

"What's a chickie run?" she asked.

"I really need to let you see that James Dean film," Drap said with a slight smile. "In *Rebel*, Jim and Buzz race at night, heading for the edge of a cliff. The first one to jump out of his vehicle is called a chicken. In the movie, Jim makes it, but Buzz gets his jacket caught on the door handle and goes over the cliff."

Sylenshia shudder. She asked, "What's a chicken?"

"I looked it up. It was an ugly bird that Earthlings raised for food, both their eggs and their carcass."

Sylenshia made a face as if she was appalled.

"We raise something similar," Drap said.

"I know, but when it's pointed out in that manner it's sort of disgusting. It bothers you to be called a chicken?"

Drap shrugged his shoulders in response. Sylenshia was bewildered and scared for Drap. He could see it in her eyes. He sighed, "It's like being called a coward."

"So?" she asked, her voice on the verge of anger and her eyes on the edge of tears.

"Look, someone's got to stand up to that wet shirt and put him in his place. I tried complimenting his ride and that didn't suffice."

"Yes, and you're already in enough trouble. Don't make it worse," she countered.

"At any rate, instead of a cliff, we'll be racing towards the Eldritch Monolith. It just seems scary. I don't think it will be that big a deal. But, I would like you to stay here instead, just in case things get out of hand."

Sylenshia's eyes blazed with fury. Her lips tightened and her nose scrunched up. Drap noticed her beautiful, fine hairs were all standing on end and her antennae were rapidly vibrating.

"The ring is dangerous and so is Klarg. I'm not letting you go up there and be ambushed by those thugs. And, I'll go where I want, Drap Vurnorj!"

Drap took a step back. He found Sylenshia's outburst extremely intimidating. Her eyes were full of rage and her jaw was tightly clenched. He gulped, forcing a lump down his throat. "Sylenshia, it's no place for a girl," Drap pleaded. "Especially the one I love."

Sylenshia momentarily paused, halting the verbal beating she was about to unleash on him. She pulled Drap close and kissed him passionately.

"That's the first time you've ever said you loved me."

"I've always loved you," Drap admitted.

"I know. I've been able to sense it, but you've never actually said it. I love you, too, which is why I can't allow you to go up there on your own."

"I'll have the guys with me."

Sylenshia laughed and then apologized. "Sorry, I didn't mean to laugh. Look, sweetie, no offense but I can take care of myself better than any of your other friends. I wish Xorbash wasn't working with my dad this evening, or I'd bring him along as well. He's helping dad refurbish mom's kitchen. Now that I've got a little extra money to spend, I bought her some new appliances she has been wanting for quite some time. She immediately put my dad and brother to work."

Drap smiled. It made him feel good, once again, that some of the changes he helped bring to the moon helped his friends and was making people happy. He liked Sylenshia's parents, and they liked him even before he came into his growing fortune. But now, his fame and fortune were bringing the bad with the good, and he needed to deal with it.

"Are you sure you won't stay?"

"No, Drap. You'll take me with you or I'll hunt you down in my plain ol' shuttle and race you there myself."

"Yeah, your plain ol' high end-shuttle. So when are you going to turn that heap into a smoking machine?"

"I will keep my shuttle as is. Now, I am the different one. Besides, Judy is enough for the two of us when I need my '50s fix."

They both laughed and kissed a while longer. She attempted to talk some sense into Drap, but he wouldn't give in, insisting he had to meet Klarg or he'd lose face and be dishonored. She didn't agree, but she quit trying to persuade him.

They flew to Bok's to grab a bite to eat and relax a moment. "Leader of the Pack" was playing. They got their food, but there was no respite as the word had spread about the chickie run. Customers pointed at Drap and Sylenshia. Some teens came over to ask if the race news was true, or if Drap was really going to show up. Would he really give away Judy if he lost? What changes would he make to the Dark Goat if he won it?

Even Brund came over to his shuttle, a determined look on her face. "What are you thinking, kid? Ya got space dust for brains?"

"I've got to do it, Brund. It's the only way he'll ever let me be."

"Oh, mz'bah droppings," she replied. "You're out of school soon. He'll go his way—prison, more than likely—and you'll be too busy running your corporation to have to worry about lowlifes like Klarg. Otherwise, you're liable to get yourself killed. Is it worth that risk? You've got a business that just keeps growing

65

and a beautiful girl at your side. Get married; have furry, multi-colored kids. Forget this stupid race and live to be old and happy like me. Well, happy. I ain't old, yet," she said with a thrust of her finger in their direction.

Both Sylenshia and Drap were a bit shocked to hear Brund mention marriage and kids.

"In case you don't listen to me," she said, still pointing her finger right in his face, "then beat the socks off of him and come back safe and sound, or I'll kill you myself once you're all better." She turned and left, heading back to the kitchen. The chorus to "American Pie" came through the PA system.

Drap knew the orange ring known as V'fin was dangerous. Millions of silicon carbide, chondrite, iron, sulfur, nickel and polyformaldehyde particles ranging from the size of molecules to boulder-sized floated within the icy ring. The radiation from the ring was low but still too dangerous to enter without the proper shielding. Most standard moon shuttles or cruisers like the transports everyone had been modifying weren't equipped to handle that sort of radiation. Maybe the additional parts added to the vehicles would deflect some of the radiation and protect the passengers, but anyone who went out that far to watch the race would need to fly through a wash station before re-entering Zardün. That was assuming that the solar winds didn't smash onlookers and racers alike into the side of an asteroid or each other.

"Last chance," Drap said as he finished his drink.

"You're right, you can stay right here where it's nice and safe," Sylenshia said. Her tone was neutral but her words were serious.

"You know that's not what I meant. You can catch a ride back home from here if you'd prefer or I could rush you back. I've got to fill up and start for V'fin in a bit."

"And I'm going with you," Sylenshia said. She leaned over, preparing to kiss him once more. She stopped short. "Well, drat. Steel yourself for a lame attempt at intimidation."

Drap looked out his optiport and saw the Dark Goat exiting the chamber. Beside him was another one of Klarg's cronies named Zrek in a replica of a '65 Barracuda Formula S. It was cherry red with a single wide, white stripe dividing it from front to back. A black scorpion emblem was painted on both portals.

Drap understood the significance of the symbol, recalling another Earth film. Despite the pending violence that was about to happen, a little piece of his mind couldn't help but think why they didn't model their shuttle after a sleek, fast, early 21st-century car called Scorpion that he remembered from his research. Oh well, when dealing with pawns and idiots...

Klarg floated the Dark Goat behind Drap, blocking him in. The Ynglasqlan stepped out of his machine and strutted over to Judy. Drap had also stepped out of his machine and stood quietly, arms crossed, eyeing his opponent. Sylenshia slid out and moved around Judy to stand by Drap's side. They watched the other greasers getting out behind Klarg, some slicking their hair back and Sklarn playing with a blade.

"I figured I'd catch you here, loser, whining to your tramp of a mixed breed."

Sylenshia hissed. Drap clenched his fist.

"You're cruisin' for a bruisin' again, loudmouth," Drap spat, his skin turning a deep purple and his eyes glowing red.

"You coming to V'fin or am I gonna have to drag your sorry carcass there myself? I'll do it, you know? Even if I have to strap you down over the hood."

"Don't worry yourself, Klarg. I'll be there. I was just enjoying a meal before your stench took away my appetite."

A few of the onlookers gathered nearby laughed at the remark.

Klarg snarled.

His boys began swiftly moving forward as two of Klarg's tentacles whipped upwards; ready to come down in a slashing stroke across Drap's neck and shoulders.

Sylenshia's hands shot out in front of her, one towards Klarg and one towards the approaching greasers. Klarg was caught in mid-swing, grunting as he was brought to an abrupt halt. The other four gang members were slammed backward, landing hard upon the parking lot, leaving them groaning in pain. Sklarn had blood trickling from his nose from hitting the invisible force Sylenshia had thrown up.

The gangsters found they couldn't move, as if turned to stone. Bok's customers and employees were slack-jawed. Sylenshia could sense the mass confusion of everyone around.

"What in the name of Mor B'og's glyk nords did you do to them?" Drap asked.

"I'll tell you later."

She stepped up to Klarg and stared him straight in the eyes.

"He said we would be there. Now, get your trash and move your heap out of here. You're not welcome at Bok's. Next time, I will shoot you into the freezing black where you can float until the end of time," she said with a scowl.

No one doubted she meant it. To prove her point, and without making a move, Klarg and his gang all levitated into the air. She held them there for a few seconds before spinning them around and dropping them back to the hard surface.

There was no laughter from any of Bok's patrons; only a few whispers could be heard. Before them stood a beautiful female, whom many had known simply as a fantasy-inducing, sexy spacehop. Some of the guys who had considered making a move on her were now glad they had reconsidered, for her powers made many suddenly afraid, not to mention a bit insecure.

Klarg scrambled up and brushed himself off. He kept a fearful eye on Sylenshia as he backed his way to the Dark Goat without a word. His gang all raced back to Zrek's shuttle, telling each other to get out of the way as they dove in and slammed their portals. Klarg spun his machine around, trying to look cool, almost hitting a pole in the process. He cut back to the left and the laser-eye hood ornament almost smacked into the Barracuda.

Klarg blasted his roaring horn. The on-lookers could hear him cursing his gang members as he motioned for them to let him pass.

Once the Scorpions were in the pressure chamber and descending, the crowd went wild, cheering and laughing. Some were brave enough to approach the couple, barraging them with a slew of compliments and questions, not only about the race but interrogating Sylenshia and wanting to know what else she could do.

Drap thought she should be a superstar or a politician as she would ask a question in response to their questions. She excitedly spoke with them without really giving them an answer. Most of the crowd never realized she had circumvented their queries about her powers.

Drap finally intervened, "All right, we've got to get some go-go juice and make our way to the starting line."

"We're there for you, Drap," many of them cheered.

"I appreciate it. Just be aware, V'fin is filled with tons of debris and very high concentrations of radiation. You really shouldn't risk it. Not for me."

A barrage of boos and remarks such as "Who cares?" and "Screw radiation!" came Drap's way.

"Fine, fine! Just be careful, my friends."

He and Sylenshia got in Judy and casually made their exit to a standing ovation. The acoustic guitar intro for "Crazy Little Thing Called Love" played through Judy's speakers, just for the two of them.

HIGHWAY STAR

*B*ok's basically cleared out, all the customers wanting to witness the showdown. Even Brund gave in. She realized she'd probably have little-to-no-business until the race was over.

She flipped the switch that turned the blazing sign off and jumped in her shuttle. Fyr and Strahntoe had modified her vessel to replicate a '55 Cadillac Fleetwood Series painted Elvis Rose. It was similar to the one the hip-swinging performer had given his mother. Brund remotely locked down the chamber lift and followed the crowd, navigating past the several orbiting fragments and chunks of a destroyed moon named Rode'an. History books stated it had been the seventh moon of O' Tulp until a meteor slammed into it several eons before Brund had ever been born.

She was the last to arrive at the makeshift raceway, where she saw the majority of her customers all lined up before V'fin's perimeter. Nearly two hundred shuttles were on hand, mostly filled to capacity. She could see faces all pressed to the front windows on either side of a wide lane, which allowed for the Dark Goat and Judy to float on parade down the center. She could barely make out Sylenshia and Drap conversing from her current distance.

"By Mor B'og, can you believe how many people are here?" Sylenshia asked.

Drap just shook his head, amazed at the size of the crowd. He heard Sylenshia say something, maybe about there being somewhere between eight hundred to a thousand onlookers, but he wasn't sure. He just stared straight ahead as he drifted towards the perimeter. He heard her shouting, "No," and something else at him. He snapped out of his stupor.

"What?"

"Stop! You're about to float into the ring."

Drap reversed his thrusters and came to a hover, just inches from the particles swirling past the front of Judy. He could feel the front end wavering up and down as an electrically charged current brushed across the front of his cruiser. He backed her up a bit, evening his nose up with the Dark Goat. His communicator crackled and cut out sporadically.

"Dead Man's Curve" now played through the speakers.

She turned down the music. "Hopefully, that's not a portent."

"Hey, Drip," came Klarg's nasty voice over the communicator. Anyone else that happened to be on the same frequency could hear the details. Drap could see his evil smile as Klarg eyed them. "Through the belt and around Eldritch Monolith. First one back out of the belt in one piece and to the line is the winner."

"Fine," Drap responded dryly. He added nothing to it and switched off his communicator. He turned the music back up. "Last Kiss" was playing.

"I should've picked a better playlist for the race. These songs are all about death and vehicles. What were those morbid Earthlings thinking?"

Sylenshia smiled and gave him a kiss like none other. She held him tight for an extra moment before whispering in his ear, "That won't be the last kiss. Now show that blowhard what you and Judy can do."

Drap felt his body tingle. He smiled as she sat back and buckled in. He saw Fyr's tailfins with bright blue dots over the tail-

71

lights spinning his shuttle around 180° and bringing his nose about to face the racers. He had a sleek starship for a hood ornament with electric blue lightning streaks racing down each side. Real lights were embedded inside the ornament, flashing like a storm. Fyr raised his communicator up so Klarg and Drap could see it.

Drap turned his communicator back on.

Fyr's voice came over, "Can you both hear me?"

Klarg flipped him an offensive tentacle.

Drap gave him a thumb's up. "I was beginning to wonder."

"Sorry about that. It took some time and planning to sneak out and pick everyone up."

"Can the sob story, you pack of wienies," Klarg ordered.

This time, Lamtan pressed all four of his hands to the front window of Fyr's Bel air and returned Klarg's gesture.

"I'll flash my lights for a three count," Fyr said, "When they light up the third time, punch it."

Drap could see Lamtan, M'Kal and even Strahntoe next to Fyr, peering out the window at him. He gave them another thumb's up."

"Come on you candy asses," Klarg said over the communicator. "You can all hug if you make it out of the belt. Make sure you have some friends still around to give you a lift back moon side, Drip, because I'm gonna kick you and your pet outta that black heap after I win."

"Do you think he realizes that if he exited his shuttle to do anything he'd die in a matter of seconds?" Sylenshia asked Drap.

Drap shrugged his shoulders. "Maybe I should invite him to try it right now. Who knows, he might fall for it."

They both looked at Klarg as he glowered back at them. Drap gave him a friendly wave and Sylenshia blew him a kiss before laying a big, fat kiss on Drap for all to see. Flashing lights from several shuttles began strafing across Judy and the empty lane before the racers. The spectators could be seen cheering the couple on. Drap saw nothing but blinding ghost images through his closed eyelids as he enjoyed the lip lock.

She pulled back and looked him square in the eyes. "Beat him off the line, Drap."

"Sure thing, my little good luck charm."

They looked back at Fyr, over to Klarg, and back to Fyr.

Hands and tentacles were gripping tightly on controllers. Beads of sweat rolled down their faces and bodies. Their teeth and jaws were clenched to the point of breaking.

FLASH!
FLASH!!
FLASH!!!

If the roar of the thrusters and burners could have been heard in space, it would've rattled the bones and threatened to burst the eardrums of the crowd. The onlookers cheered as brilliant blasts of fire erupted from the rear of both Judy and Dark Goat while the vessels streaked across the starting line and zipped past Fyr's '57 Chevy, straight into the debris of the belt.

Judy managed to get the jump on Dark Goat, leading by four lengths. Klarg began to catch up as the racers dodged the larger obstacles swirling before them, threatening to bust through their windows. Both pilots had to hold tight to the yoke of their shuttles to keep the solar winds from rolling them over or slamming them into another object. Bits of ice and debris obscured their vision, making the race even dicier than either had considered.

It would be a couple of more minutes before they saw the Eldritch Monolith. It was a humongous asteroid chunk that looked a bit like the evil, misshapen face of an angry god. If it ever escaped the ring's orbit and hit a moon, it would destroy all life upon the doomed body, leaving it looking much like Rode'an.

"He's catching up, Drap," Sylenshia said, her voice slightly stressed. She had Drap's optical magnifiers to keep track of Klarg.

"I know. The debris is getting larger and denser. Hold on," Drap yelled as he pulled up hard to avoid a tumbling cluster headed straight for Sylenshia's portal. It went whizzing beneath him, rocking Judy and nearly flipping her. Sylenshia reported that it ripped the skull hood ornament off of the Dark Goat.

"I bet he jettisoned his bowels on that one," Drap said with a chuckle. "There it is," he said, pointing out what appeared to be a small asteroid, but was quickly looming larger. "We'll be there in another five minutes or so."

Debris particles were shooting past them, rocking the cruiser once more, scuffing the windshield and stripping the paint job. The *pings* damaging the exterior could be heard within. Drap's knuckles were white. The rest of him was a constant change of colors as he gripped the controls, maneuvering through the ring. Sylenshia had momentarily stopped watching Klarg once Drap had mentioned the Eldritch Monolith.

"Drap," she said excitedly, "coming from below on my side. It's a huge meteorite heading straight for us. It's moving really fast."

Drap checked over his shoulder and saw Klarg just a little ways behind him, maybe a quarter mile distant. The Monolith was just seconds away now. He still couldn't see the meteorite with his own eyes, but he could see it hurtling at them on his radar, which was screaming a red alert.

"Hold tight and brace yourself," Drap said firmly. He quickly wiped his left hand then his right against his shirt and got a new grip on the yoke as he prepared for a move he had never before attempted.

He flipped a clear lid up that shielded a large, red button on his control panel. He smacked the button with the palm of his hand. Judy shot forward so fast that both Drap and Sylenshia felt as if they were going to technospew all over the shuttle's interior.

Instead of swinging portside around the Eldritch Monolith as they raced towards the towering behemoth, Drap dipped below the obstacle, unable to dodge the smaller pieces dragged by its gravitational pull. Several fist-sized pieces and larger hunks of matter slammed into Judy. The Monolith seemed to also be the border of where the ice really began to build up. It was getting more difficult to see as condensation crystallized across Judy's window. Drap had to rely solely on his radar as he waited for the right moment to pull up and slingshot over the top of the Eldritch Monolith. There was so much debris and ice he could no longer tell where the speeding meteorite had disappeared to that had been on a trajectory straight for them.

"Drap?" Sylenshia questioned nervously. Her nails were digging deep into his leg and the armrest.

"Almost there. Can you ease up on the death grip? Your drawing blood."

"Sorry about that," she said, disconcerted as she pulled her nails out of him. There was some blood under her nails and on his clothing, but they had bigger things to worry about at the moment.

Drap saw his clearing and pulled up hard, climbing in a vertical arc. They could look out of the top of the ship, barely able to see the rugged wall through the frost as they went higher and higher. The velocity was pulling so many G's that Drap and Sylenshia's lips were pulling back into a rictus grin. Drap could finally see light reflecting off Zardün and creeping over the top of the Monolith. He topped the massive killer and barrel-rolled twice until he came back to an upright orientation – the Eldritch Monolith now in a position below Judy. Drap aimed for Zardün.

"Oh, Mor B'og, I'm going to be sick," said Sylenshia, her face pale even through her fur, which was standing on end, and her eyes were fully dilated. She had a hand to her stomach.

Drap quickly risked taking a hand off the yoke, patting her leg twice then grasping the yoke once more. "No worries, my classy chassis. We're all done with—oh, no!"

Sylenshia looked at the radar and was aghast, seeing what Drap was reacting to on the screen. She knew Drap needed to concentrate and keep his hands on the controls. She took the initiative and reached for the switch on the communicator.

"Klarg, this is Sylenshia. Don't argue. Just listen. A meteorite is headed straight on a collision course for the Monolith. We can't see where you are, but if you are maneuvering around it, just keep going. Do not, I repeat, do not try to swing around the Monolith. Do–not—swing around the Monolith."

"I ain't falling for your lame trick and I ain't giving up, mixed breed. I'll have you dipsticks back in my sites in a nanosecond."

"Don't be a lorkor brain! Shoot clear of the Monolith before..."

Sylenshia was unaware the rest of her warning went unheard by Klarg. He switched his communicator off so he could concentrate. He looked down at his radar and saw the large obstacle that was on a collision course for the Monolith. He turned his head and looked out the icy port side of the Dark Goat. He had flown around the Monolith's girth instead of the under and over maneuver he had considered a bonehead move by Drap. Now he knew why, because Judy would've been right in the meteorite's path if Drap had swung starboard around the Monolith's girth.

The meteorite was colossal and tumbling fast. Its awkward trajectory made it difficult to tell just where it was going to lay its path of destruction. Klarg was certain he was going to be in that path.

"Grrrr!" he yelled.

He didn't want to admit to himself Sylenshia had been right. He punched it and gave the Dark Goat all she had. He also had an injection booster that he planned to save for the final leg of the race. Now he wished he had hit it to round the Monolith.

He pulled up and twisted the injector handle to boost his shuttle but nothing happened. He slammed it back into place and then repeated his actions, pulling and twisting. Still nothing. He slammed it back down and pulled once more, this time twisting the handle so sharply that he wrenched the metal apart. The booster failed and never kicked in.

Klarg screamed as he watched his imminent killer toppling towards him. He didn't even have time for his short life to flash before his eyes as the meteorite crashed into him, carrying bits and pieces of the Dark Goat and Klarg with it as the destructor made impact, exploding against the Eldritch Monolith, near a segment that resembled a snarling mouth.

The force of the collision blasted both giants apart. Gas, debris and pieces of Klarg exploded with the power of several bombs. The shockwave rippled, swallowing up everything in its way and spitting it back out. More explosions erupted from thousands of smaller collisions.

Drap watched his radar. They dared not look out the ports and be blinded by the eruptions. His extra booster had used itself up. Judy had no tricks left. It was going to be a close call to get out of the V'fin Belt before the shockwave and shower of debris rained down on them and, with any luck, not through them.

"What an awful way to go," Sylenshia said. "I know he was a jerk, but—Oh, I hope the others are getting clear."

Drap was worried about all those back at the finish line, but he tried to be positive. "I'm sure they're seeing the explosion and heading away to safety."

Sylenshia looked at him as she placed a comforting hand on his forearm. "It's okay to be worried, but I appreciate you trying to comfort me."

"Yeah, right. You can sense when I'm full of it."

She smiled, "I love you, Drap. Now get us out of here, you big dope. I know you and Judy can do it."

Drap made the straightest beeline he could. He had Judy fully opened up, giving her all he could. He patted her illuminated dash with a sweaty palm.

"Come on, girl. I know you've got it in you. Don't let us down."

"There's the edge of the belt. Almost everyone is out of sight," Sylenshia said breathlessly.

Judy burst through the perimeter and crossed what would've been the finish line. Drap didn't slow down. He was approaching the last shuttle in the long line of escaping transports. It was Brund's pink Cadillac that Judy caught up with as the wave flowed into the back of the gullwing hybrid.

Microscopic to pebble-sized particles scraped down the sides of the cruiser past them. They could feel Judy shift and rock fiercely, throwing her into an uncontrollable spin. If it hadn't been for the five-point belts Drap had installed, they would have been battered and bruised from banging about the shuttle's interior.

Drap gave up attempting to master the cruiser as they were tossed end over end. He grabbed Sylenshia's hand and conquered his feelings, overcoming the fear and just exuding his love for her. She picked up on his emotions. Despite their immediate danger, she relaxed. His love was like inhaling sweet flowers on a summer day after a light rain. It made her feel good all over. She overcame her fear.

It seemed like they had been spinning and tumbling forever. When they finally slowed and eventually came adrift, they were flipped over, floating in a position between Drap's side and upside down according to the onboard computer. Drap tried the controls and found Judy responded. He got her upright once more.

Drap didn't realize his hand had brushed the volume control switch. "All Shook Up" could be faintly heard. The couple looked at one another, each laughing softly at the coincidence. Drap unstrapped his safety harness and moved closer to Sylenshia as she got free of her harness. He kissed her. They pulled closer and held one another tightly.

Lost in their own little world, they were finally interrupted by an array of lights flashing all around them. Fyr and many others had backtracked to make certain Drap and Sylenshia had survived. Even Brund was there, a smile across her cherubic face as she applauded, bouncing like an excited child in her seat. Drap and Sylenshia turned and waved to everyone. They tried the communicator, but there was too much radiation and debris in the vicinity to get a signal.

"I'm in the mood for a hot fudge sundae after all of that excitement," said Drap. He gave Sylenshia one more peck on the lips. He then kissed his fingertips before patting Judy's console. "Way to go girls."

Sylenshia pointed to Brund, signaling to her they were heading back to Bok's. It took her a moment, but Brund caught on and nodded enthusiastically.

Drap throttled forward at a comfortable cruising speed, Brund on one side of him and Fyr on the other. His buddies were all up in the front of the '57, singing along to some rockin' song and having a great time. A convoy spread out behind them, following in their wake, eager to greet and congratulate them—not on the win, but on being alive."

The party at Bok's went on through the night, the bubble encapsulating it a bit pockmarked from the aftermath of the explosion. Everyone took inventory of the damage each shuttle had sustained. None appeared as skinned up and damaged as Judy, at least none other as badly if the Dark Goat wasn't included in the equation. Later, they would discover most of the small meteoroids burned up before making it to Zardün's surface.

Judy was definitely going to need some work, but she'd be fit to fly again in no time. Drap sat Sylenshia on the hood and dropped to a knee. So many emotions from the crowd were bombarding Sylenshia all at once from her friends and former co-workers that she missed seeing the brilliant red Pleisian's action. She didn't know if they were happy she was alive or excited about the race. She failed to pick up on what Drap was about to do until the words were out of his mouth.

She looked down into his eyes. She sensed his proposal wasn't totally a spur of the moment thing, but something that had been building deep within and planned, although maybe not tonight, but sometime soon.

"Yes," she replied.

She pulled him into a standing position and there, in front of everyone, the engaged couple kissed.

Brund quickly pulled up a music file. "Earth Angel (Will You Be Mine)" played. Drap and Sylenshia danced in the center court of Bok's. The crowd remained silent for the most part, discounting a sob or two from a girl here and there, watching the couple have their moment.

The next tune in the queue was "When a Man Loves a Woman." Other couples joined the lovebirds as the adventurous night turned to a wondrous day.

★ ★ ★

Fl' k and the other greasers stared up into space. The belt was much denser after the explosion, particles blasted into a million more particles and releasing various gasses. Each of them strained to find a way to secretly wipe away their tears, trying not to lose their cool.

They stood before an impromptu memorial they'd made for Klarg Dyklor, gathering rocks that took two hands to lift and carry. The gang felt lost as they formed the stones in the shape of the first letters of his name on the edge of a cliff overhanging the Norganti River. It was a secret place they used to chill and just be themselves when they didn't have to act tough around others. Klarg loved the view and peacefulness, even if he'd never admit it out loud.

"Now what, Fl' k?" Sklarn asked.

He looked at the sad bunch about him. He shook his head and said, "School's over in a week. I think after that I'll go to Jen-Dale for a vacation, maybe see about a job with Rock 'N' Moon, Inc. Later gators."

Fl' k squirmed out of his faux leather jacket and laid it on the memorial, the scorpion symbol facedown. He turned and walked away as dawn kissed the horizon.

ABOUT THE AUTHOR

Ethan Nahté grew up collecting albums and music magazines instead of Hot Wheels and G.I. Joe. He hit the stage at an early age, performing in his first play by second grade, then the church choir by third grade, including a live radio broadcast as the co-lead vocalist. He also danced onstage, being the only boy in his dance class with several girls. This was around the same time when Disco was popular and he didn't know any better (about the music, not the girls). By age 10 he had his first drum set. He played percussion in marching band & concert band starting at age 12. He began playing in rock bands by the time he was 13. He had his first synthesizers by 14 and guitars by age 15. He was accepted to a handful of music colleges upon graduation from high school but, unfortunately, never attended.

In addition to the school band, Ethan performed in several amateur & semi-professional bands throughout the '80s and '90s. The multi-instrumentalist played classic rock, heavy metal, hard rock, both country & western (gotta get the Blues Brothers in there), some oldies, as well as new age. He has performed in clubs, concert halls, on outdoor stages, the steps of a courthouse on a snowy day, churches, and amphitheaters.

Ethan also composed music for TV programs, radio spots & short indie films. For several years he produced his own music television programs: *LIVE 'N' LOUD* and *SoundScapes*, featuring local acts as well as many national acts. In addition, he was a professional photo-journalist for several music & entertainment publications around the globe, interviewing & reviewing many of his idols & favorite bands from the late '60s and onward. He spent many nights at the front of the stage, letting the music flow through him—taking him away to a much better place.

ABOUT THE ARTIST

Brad W. Foster, international jet-setter and ex-secret agent, sometimes dabbles in pen and ink. This tends to get him very dirty, and his friends avoid him at all the "right" clubs. However, other times he uses a pen almost correctly and makes strange little pictures on paper. These have somehow managed to make their way into the hands of various publishers of, appropriately enough, various publications. This has resulted, at the last count, in his work having been published in literally over 3,000 diverse books, magazines, posters, prints, cards, and a little of everything else!

Aside from the hundreds of science fiction fanzines to have used his work, magazines as broad-ranging in subjects as *Amazing Stories*, *Highlights for Children*, and *Cavalier* have carried his illustrations. (The man is nothing if not diverse in his choice of subjects!) He has illustrated computer instruction books, a children's picture book, an over-sized coloring album, advertising posters, role-playing games, book covers, comic books, and much more.

He has started up and is still running his own small press publishing house, Jabberwocky Graphix, from which he issues a line of fine-art prints and art collections. He and his lovely wife Cindy travel around the country to show his work at various juried art festivals, as well as science fiction and comic conventions, cat shows, and they even participated in a two-month Renaissance Festival deep in the heart of Texas for eight years, though he eventually got over that.

Brad will draw for just about any reason or excuse, and found in science fiction fandom a group of folks who welcomed his output of odd illustrations and cartoons. Artworks done purely for the enjoyment of the creation of the work, with no thought toward "payment", found the perfect home in SF fandom. And not only have these folks been kind enough to print his weird doodles and then send him free copies of those magazines, they've also been nice enough to bestow eight Hugo awards on him for, basically, just having fun. He hopes to move on to new worlds with his art—he and Cindy are slowly developing a huge cast of characters for a new project that will combine his fine art and comic-book sides, and there are always new prints and strange art projects planned through Jabberwocky Graphix. But in the meantime, and for all time, he'll continue to draw whenever he can, just for the fun of it.

His motto says it all: "Leave no piece of paper blank!"

Made in the USA
Middletown, DE
07 June 2022

66703403R00056